TONY AND ME

Other Books by Alfred Slote

TONY AND ME

by Alfred Slote

J. B. LIPPINCOTT COMPANY

PHILADELPHIA AND NEW YORK

U.S. Library of Congress Cataloging in Publication Data

Slote, Alfred.
  Tony and me.

  SUMMARY: Tony, a star athlete, befriends Bill and gives hope
to the losing baseball team, but Tony's problems force Bill to make
some tough decisions.
  [1. Baseball—Fiction.   2. Shoplifting—Fiction.   3. Friend-
ship—Fiction] I. Title.
PZ7.S635To   [Fic]   74-5182
ISBN-0-397-31507-4

This one's for Ben

TONY AND ME

1

MOVING FROM one place to another is no good. You have to make new friends, check out new schools, get onto new ball clubs.

Last year when my father announced that we were going to leave California and move to Michigan, I was really upset.

"Why do we have to do that?"

"Because the company wants me to be the assistant manager of their store in Arborville, Michigan."

"You're an assistant manager here. Why do you have to do the same thing in Michigan?"

Dad laughed. "Bill, you make Michigan sound like the end of the earth. It isn't. Just to start with, Arborville is a college town. Secondly, it's only for one year. The assistant manager there is going to New York for a year. Thirdly, being an assistant manager there isn't the same as being one here, because the Arborville store is a lot bigger than ours. Fourth, unless I'm prepared to quit and find a new job, which I'm not, I'm going to do what the company tells me to do. Those are the facts of life, Bill, and that's the end of the discussion."

And it was. Which is what it's like to be a kid. You can have all the family discussions you want. But when it gets to the end, you go where your parents want to go. And we went to Michigan.

Last spring we arrived in Arborville. Mom got me enrolled in the fifth grade of Sampson Park School and Dad got me onto a kids' baseball team. It wasn't official Little League in Arborville. It was their version of it, and a pretty poor version it was.

There were no real ball parks, no fences, no advertising, no dugouts. Just city park baseball with parents sitting around in plastic lawn chairs, gossiping with each other or hollering at their own kids.

The whole thing was pretty bush. Even that would have been tolerable if I'd got onto a decent team. But the team I got on—the ten-year-old entry from the Sampson Park neighborhood—was the Miller Laundry team, and they were a bunch of clowns.

We finished in last place in our division of the ten-year-old league last year. I played hard (the only way I know how to play), hit well, fielded well. But we had no pitcher, no team leader, and what our coach, Mr. Benz, knew about baseball could fill up half a thimble. Half a small thimble.

It was pretty discouraging. The only thing that

kept me going all fall and winter was knowing that this June we'd be going home to California. My big occupation that winter was to lie on my bed and count cracks in the ceiling. I'd try to find a crack for every day we had left before we went home. By the first of June, I was down to looking for nineteen cracks.

And then one rainy afternoon after school I was down to fifteen. In fact, I'd just finished ticking off fifteen cracks when my mother called up the stairs.

"Bill, what're you doing up there?"

"Nothing."

"Don't you have a baseball practice at the park this afternoon?"

"It's raining, Mom."

I could hear the rain running in the gutters over my bedroom window. What did she expect?

"I know that, Bill Taylor. But the team is supposed to meet to help Mr. Benz draft players for this season."

"Yeah, but I don't know any of the other guys in the league. I'm only going to be here for one official game. I'm not even getting a new uniform."

"You get over there anyway. Right now you're still part of that team, and if the team is meeting, you meet with them."

Mom's strict. There's a right way and a wrong way to do something, and you better do it the right way and do it fast.

"So go!" she said.

I got. I hopped off the bed, got my glove and shoes from my closet floor, and went downstairs. She was waiting for me at the foot of the stairs. She didn't trust me.

"If there's anything dumber than lying in bed in the middle of the afternoon, I don't know what it is," she said.

"I do."

"What?"

"Playing baseball in the rain."

She swatted at me. I ducked, laughing, and went outside.

"Bill," Mom called.

I turned.

A warm-up jacket came flying out the door and landed on my nose. "That'll keep you dry behind the ears," she said, grinning. "Have fun."

"Impossible," I said.

"Try," she said, and shut the door.

I shook my head in disbelief. Have fun playing baseball with a team like the Miller Laundries? Only a mother who knew nothing about baseball could say a thing like that.

I walked through the rain to Sampson Park.

2

THE PARK was deserted. The only person I could see was a man with an umbrella walking his dog. He was holding the umbrella over the dog. And they say Californians are crazy!

"Hey, Bill, we're over here."

The shout came from the shelter near the basketball court. I saw them then, clowning around under the overhang, the Miller Laundry team. Just by looking at those guys—some of them in T-shirts, others in sweat shirts (they never wore their uniforms in practice the way we did in California, pridefully)—just by looking at them you could tell they didn't believe in themselves. No wonder guys on other teams greeted us with: "Hey, Laundries, we're gonna whitewash you." Or, "Hey, Laundries, we're gonna knock the starch out of you." Or, "Hey, Laundries, we're gonna hang you up to dry."

Tired old taunts. Every team trotted them out as

13

though they'd just made them up. I couldn't blame them, really. We acted like a bunch of clowns.

We had only three real ball players on the team: Doc Overmeyer, the catcher; Willie Soames, who played first base; and me, who played shortstop. I'm not bragging. I'm just stating a fact. Everyone else was awful. Plus we had no pitcher. The guys spent the winter hoping the team would be dissolved so they could be drafted onto better teams. But the only time they broke up a team was if it lost its coach and sponsor or couldn't get at least fourteen guys to start the season with. Mr. Benz, unfortunately, went on coaching. Miller Laundry, not realizing the bad publicity it was getting from the box scores, went on sponsoring, and most of the guys were too lazy to quit. So now we were supposed to have a meeting and a practice. We were meeting to advise Mr. Benz on what players he should draft from another team that had had the sense to get itself dissolved. I couldn't have cared less. We were going back to California where we belonged. The Miller Laundry baseball team could draft, dissolve, or die, for all I cared.

"Come on, Bill, we're waiting on you," Roger Martilla called out. Roger was team captain, not because he was a good ball player—he wasn't—but because he was willing to call up guys to make sure they knew where the game was and that they had a ride to it. He was more a clerk than a captain,

14

but Mr. Benz appointed him captain last year because, as Mr. Benz put it, "Roger cares."

"It'd be better if he didn't care so much and hit better," Stan Pecora, our second baseman, grumbled, but everyone privately agreed that a lousy team might just as well have a lousy captain and it wasn't worth making a stir about.

The trouble was that Roger took his job seriously and was always ordering people around.

"Hump it, Bill," Roger called out to me.

"Hump it yourself," I yelled back.

"Get a move on, Bill," Mr. Benz called.

You move for a coach, even a bad coach. I broke into a trot. And then the wisecracks started.

"Hey, it runs."

"On regular or premium?"

"Nifty-thrifty."

"Two bucks on Taylor to place."

"Where do you play, Bill? Defensive tackle?"

"He's our shortstop? Man, are we in trouble!"

"All right," Mr. Benz's voice boomed out. "Knock off the chatter. We've got some important work to do."

Mr. Benz, a big horse-faced man, embarrassed his son Allie most of the time. Allie pitched for us, badly. Mr. Benz had never played much baseball himself. He was always saying things like: "Got to get good wood on it." Or, "You can hit him, just swing sooner." Real, specific, helpful advice. But when you asked him how to hook slide around a tag, he'd always say that one of these days he'd get in a sliding specialist to show us.

Once, Jack Berberian asked him with a straight face if they didn't used to slide when he played ball.

"Not much, Jack," Mr. Benz said. "We always sort of plowed right in."

After that, whenever we had a guy stealing or trying to stretch a hit, we always shouted: "Plow right in."

We plowed all right. We plowed our way right into last place and stayed there, plowed under.

"All right, boys. Gather round me. I've got a list of names."

"What team's breaking up, Mr. Benz?" Stan Pecora asked.

"The Weston Gravel team from the other division."

"Why didn't they break us up instead?" Harry Heymann, our center fielder, asked. Heymann was considered the team comedian, though I thought he had a lot of good competition.

"Shut up, Heymann," said Terry Driscoll, our left fielder. "Let's hear who's up for grabs."

"That's right," Mr. Benz said, and adjusted his glasses as he looked over his paper. "What we do here right now might make the difference between a winning season and a losing one. Because we finished in last place in our division, we have a chance to get first pick in the draft tonight."

"What about the team that finished last in the other division?" Jack Berberian asked. Jack was the team thinker and a poor right fielder.

"We're going to flip with them," Mr. Benz said.

"So we might not get first pick," Pecora said.

"That's right," Mr. Benz said, "but I haven't lost a coin flip in years."

He could say funny things, all right. He should have been coaching a team of coin flippers.

"Well," Heymann said, "I finally know why we played so badly last year. To get a chance to pick first."

"You're not funny, Heymann," Roger Martilla said.

"Shut up, everyone," Driscoll said. "What's the first name on the list, Mr. Benz?"

"The list's in alphabetical order, and the first name is Aker. John Aker. Who knows him? Anyone?"

"Yeah," Doc Overmeyer grunted. "I know him."

"Any good?"

"He stinks."

Doc never wasted words.

"Isn't he the big red-headed guy, Doc?" Pecora asked.

"Naw, that's Wolfe."

"Wolfe doesn't have red hair."

"Sure he does."

"Wanna bet?"

"Aw, shut up," Roger Martilla said. "Here we are trying to draft ball players, and you guys are arguing about red hair."

"Who're you telling to shut up?" Doc asked softly.

"I'm just saying we ought to be quiet," Roger mumbled. "I can't hear Mr. Benz."

I laughed. Roger gave me a hurt look. Mr. Benz just looked saddened by it all.

"Boys," he said, "the sooner we get through this list and pick our people, the sooner we get out on the old diamond."

"It's raining on the old diamond, Mr. Benz," Jack Berberian said.

"A little water won't hurt you any, Jack," Mr. Benz said, smiling. "Why, in the old days we used to play baseball games in the mud."

"What *was* it like in the old days, Mr. Benz?" Heymann asked solemnly.

Mr. Benz laughed. He was good-natured, all right. "Now, Harry, don't get me started on the old days. We've got work at hand. Aker's no good, then."

"He's terrible," Doc said.

"All right. The next name on the list is Crawford. Don Crawford. Anyone know him?"

"I do," Driscoll said. "He's their shortstop."

"Hey, we'll need a shortstop when Taylor goes."

"We'll need a shortstop even if Taylor stays."

"Bill, are you really going to California?"

I looked at those clowns and thought: *The sooner the better.*

"What do you want to go there for, man? They got earthquakes there."

"And smog."

"And forest fires."

"And mud slides."

"And—"

"And will you guys shut up?" Roger yelled, and his voice almost broke. "It may stop raining, and we can get some practice in."

"Who needs practice?" Heymann asked.

That broke everyone up. Morale on this team was at an all-time low. When a team laughs at itself, you know it's all through. I hoped it would go on raining.

"Boys," Mr. Benz said, "we all need practice, and I'll tell you something more. I've booked us a practice game for Monday against Michigan Pharmacy."

"The Pharmacy?" Heymann said. "Mr. Benz, they'll kill us."

"We never got more than one run off those guys in two years," said Lew Mira, a left-handed pitcher.

"Let's fool them and forfeit," Heymann said.

"You can't forfeit a practice game, Heymann."

"*We* can. We can do anything."

Mr. Benz lost his patience. "Let's cut it out now. The game is set for this park Monday at four thirty. If you're scared to play, let me know, and I'll cross you off the team roster. Right now we're here to find a player we want from the Weston Gravel team. Don Crawford's a shortstop. I'll put a mark next to his name. With Bill Taylor leaving, maybe Crawford's our best bet. The next name on the list is Ed Filippo."

"No good. Definitely."

"Bernard Groggins."

"He's worse."

"Boy, they sound as bad as we are."

"No, they don't."

"Bob Isaacs?"

"Berberian knows him. They play chess together."

Jack Berberian nodded. "He's a good chess player." He was serious as he said it. Everyone laughed.

Jack had once let a fly ball hit him on the head. When Mr. Benz asked him what he thought he was doing out there, Jack said he had been playing a chess game in his head, and he was sorry.

"Let's draft him, Mr. Benz," Heymann said. "Jack needs someone to talk to."

"No, he doesn't," Pecora replied. "Jack can go on talking to himself."

"Boys, will you please cut it out?" Mr. Benz was beginning to look weary. I felt sorry for him. He couldn't control this team, much less lead it. He couldn't even get their attention long enough to draft a player.

"We seem to have twins next on the list. Arthur and Alan Johnson."

"Both lousy."

"Joe Mellendorfer?"

"He's their catcher. He's not bad."

"We got Doc."

"Doc don't look so good this year."

"Nuts to you, Pecora," Doc said amiably. If ever a guy was sure he was a good ball player, it was Doc Overmeyer. He would not have been a starter on my California team, though he was a big star here.

"Willie Pentland," Mr. Benz said, reading the next name on the list.

"Hey, ain't he a cousin of yours, Willie?"

Our Willie, Willie Soames, got mad. Ordinarily, Willie's hard to rattle. He takes things pretty easy. But this Willie Pentland was probably black, and so was our Willie. Maybe Pecora hadn't meant anything by it, maybe he thought they really were cousins, but Willie was mad anyway.

"He ain't no cousin of mine, Pecora. Maybe he's a cousin of yours."

No one laughed. It wasn't funny when Willie Soames got mad. Pecora backed off lightly. "Hey, man, I thought this Pentland dude and you played ball together."

"We don't."

"Sorry."

" 's OK." Willie relaxed. So did we.

Mr. Benz sighed. He didn't understand any of this. He looked down at his list. "Who knows Dave Ross?"

"I've played hockey with him," Terry Driscoll said. "He's a good hockey player."

"Maybe they'll let him bat with a curved stick."

"Heymann, how come you're not on TV?"

"I haven't been discovered yet."

"We can't wait for the day."

"Calm down, boys," Mr. Benz said, for the umpteenth time. "We're almost through the list. Clarence Ruppert."

"Terrible."

"You never heard of him, Pecora."

"With a name like Clarence, how can he be any good?"

"Ed Sanders," Mr. Benz said.

"Worse than Clarence."

"Bart Slocum?"

No one knew Bart Slocum or cared to know him. No one even pretended to know him. We were bored. The rain was stopping. It was better to throw a ball around than to gab endlessly about a bunch of guys who weren't ball players either.

"That's a real nothing team," Driscoll said. "Draft their shortstop and let's play some ball."

"Now, wait on," Mr. Benz said. "There're just a few more names. Tony Spain."

"Tony Spain!" Pecora's eyes popped.

"Holy cow."

"Grab him!"

Doc whistled. He turned to Willie Soames. "I didn't know Spain was on that team."

"I knew he played for someone."

"You boys know him?" Mr. Benz asked. If Mr. Benz was a real coach, he would have known this hotshot too. Real coaches always know what is going on with other teams. Back home, our coach, Mr. Dettling, always scouted other teams' games when we weren't playing. He was up on every player in the league. Mr. Benz had a hard time keeping up with the players on his own team.

"Mr. Benz," Heymann said, serious for once, "Tony Spain is the best baseball player our age in town."

"He pitched two no-hitters last year," Pecora said.

"He throws curves."

"Spain can hit too," Willie said, grinning. "I saw him hit a ball over the left field fence of Diamond One at Vets'."

"You're kidding."

"No. I saw it with my own eyes."

"Grab him, Mr. Benz."

"We got to win that coin flip first."

"Mr. Benz, it's up to you. If you win the coin flip, we got a winning season because Spain can do it for us."

Mr. Benz looked solemn. "Boys, I'll do my best tonight. I'll try and get us Tony Spain."

"If we get him, can he play with us Monday against the Pharmacy?"

"I don't see why not."

"Boy, I'd like to see their faces."

"What time's the coaches' meeting tonight, Mr. Benz?"

"Seven thirty."

"You better practice flipping coins."

"I don't flip them," Mr. Benz said, with a laugh. "I just call them."

"You better practice calling them, then. Let's hear you say 'Heads,' Mr. Benz."

"Boys, I'll do my best. But there are some more names on the list."

"Forget 'em. Get Spain."

"But if I can't get him?"

"Crawford, their shortstop. But get Spain. When he's not pitching, he can play short. He can play anywhere."

"All right, boys." Mr. Benz put the list down. "I'll do my best to get Tony Spain."

"Hey, let's have some practice," Heymann said.

And with that, the guys ran out from under the overhang and onto the big diamond at Sampson Park. I'd never seen them run onto a ball field before. It was the idea that they were going to land this hotshot that did it. It was funny. The worse a team got, the more it put its faith in miracles.

Tony Spain. It was a funny name for a miracle maker.

I walked onto the diamond after them.

3

HAPPINESS only lasted a little while with this team. Mr. Benz dissolved it by pitching batting practice. He couldn't get the ball over. Then he got Roger to pitch, and he gave batting tips. His batting tips were like this:

"Swing level, Jack."

"Keep your eye on the ball, Terry."

"Get ready, Willie."

Roger got one ball in five over the plate, and gradually the practice fell apart. Nothing kills the spirit faster than having to stand around in the field while your pitcher is wild and your coach takes up time saying things that don't mean anything.

When that happens, guys start fooling around. Finally, so many guys were goofing off that Mr. Benz announced that *he* would hit some balls to us.

"Allie, Jack, Terry, you'll be base runners. Allie, get over here."

I felt sorry for Allie Benz. Having a terrible

coach for a father must be the worst feeling in the world. We all liked Allie too much to kid him about it; you could see how he suffered.

Now he crouched by home plate waiting for his dad to hit the ball. This was how his dad pretended it was a real game.

"OK," Mr. Benz said, "nobody on and nobody out. Here we go."

Only we didn't go. He threw the ball up, swung, and missed. Just trying to tap a ball to the infield, he missed it. Throwing the ball up himself. It's the kind of thing that's hard to believe if you haven't seen it with your own eyes. And him a baseball coach. He laughed good-naturedly, but Allie blushed beet red.

Mr. Benz gave Roger Martilla on third a grim look. "Be alert, Captain," he said. It was his way of telling Roger that the ball was coming his way. Probably a bunt. Mr. Benz liked Roger, and he liked his captain to look good. He threw the ball up and tapped a bunt . . . foul.

Pecora laughed out loud. "Hey, maybe we better not let Tony Spain see us play. He may decide not to play baseball this year."

"Aw, shut up, Pecora," Allie said.

Mr. Benz tried again, and this time he connected. He sent an easy ground ball down the third base line. Roger hesitated, not knowing whether to charge it or not. He wasn't an instinctive third baseman. He didn't have a good arm. I think the only reason he played third was that he had told Mr. Benz his father had been a third baseman when he was a kid, and Mr. Benz had a great loyalty to the good old days.

At the last second Roger decided that if he wanted a play at first, he'd have to charge it. He did and kicked the ball.

"Field goal. Three points," Heymann called out from center. "You scared to go for the TD, Rog?"

"Shut up, Heymann," Roger said.

"You've got to play the ball, Roger," Mr. Benz said cheerfully. "Don't let the ball play you."

"Now what's that supposed to mean?" Pecora said to me, hiding his mouth behind his glove.

Pecora knew what it meant, all right. It was just that when Mr. Benz said it, it didn't mean anything.

"All right, let's try it again," Mr. Benz called out.

"Just like a real game," Pecora said, and yawned.

"You want me home, Dad?" Allie asked from first base.

Mr. Benz thought about it. "No, you stay there. All right, we've got a man on first and nobody out. Dangerous Lew Mira is up."

Lew Mira, our left-handed pitcher, crouched by the plate.

"Roger," Mr. Benz said, "look alive!"

It was the only simulated game in history in which the batter warned the fielder that the ball was coming. Mr. Benz wanted to hit the same kind of easy grounder to Roger. Allie took off on the swing. The ball sliced upward, a soft, easy liner. Roger grabbed it. Allie turned and tried to get back to first. He slipped in a muddy spot. Everyone laughed.

"Allie," Mr. Benz said, "you should have waited to see where the ball was going."

"Some days you can't trust anybody," Pecora said to me.

By this time, whatever fire Tony Spain's name had lit under the team was completely gone. More guys were goofing off, throwing wildly, arguing with each other, and Willie Soames wrote the end to it by walking off the field in disgust. Mr. Benz called it off. Half the guys hadn't hit, half hadn't handled the ball in the field. They were all bellyaching. Tony Spain would have to be a genuine miracle man to turn this team around. It would almost be worth not going to California to watch him fail.

"Gather round," Mr. Benz called. "Come on, Heymann."

One by one, with Berberian last, the guys came around the coach.

"All right, boys," he said, "it isn't a very good day for a practice at that. Tonight is what is important. The draft meeting. I'll let Roger know what happens, and he can call the rest of you. Monday afternoon at four thirty we've got a game against Michigan Pharmacy. This diamond."

"Mr. Benz, don't you think we ought to have another practice between now and Monday?"

"Well, Stan," Mr. Benz said, thinking it over, "we could have a practice tomorrow, but I'm pretty sure all the diamonds here are taken for Saturday. How many of you boys would like a practice tomorrow?"

Who ever heard of a coach asking his team if they wanted a practice? Especially a team that made a habit of finishing in last place.

Half the arms shot up. Willie, Doc, Pecora, Driscoll, Heymann, Roger . . . all the regulars. The subs, the guys who really needed practice, didn't want it.

Pecora looked at me. "What about you, Bill?"

"I don't care."

"He's dreaming about California again."

"Nuts to you, Heymann."

"Oranges, you mean."

"How about Berberian?"

Jack blinked. "What about me?"

"Can you make a practice tomorrow?"

"Practice what?" Jack asked, and that broke up the team meeting. Even Mr. Benz laughed.

A real sad team. It made more sense to stay in bed and count cracks on the ceiling than to play ball with these guys.

Roger walked my way. He was a funny, serious kid who always wanted to do right, look good, but never quite made it. He was no athlete, though he worked hard at it. He'd probably make a good team manager in high school. Now he was very quiet.

"What's up, Rog?" I asked him.

"I was thinking about the team."

"There'll be better practices."

"I wasn't thinking about that. I was thinking about Tony Spain. About the kind of difference he could make."

"I've never seen him play, so I can't tell you."

"He's good," Roger said. "He's unbelievably good. That Weston Gravel team wasn't any good, but I bet the reason they finished kind of high up was because of him. I just hate for us to be counting on one guy that much."

"Don't count on him, then."

"I hope he's nice."

"Why's he got to be nice? Nice guys finish last. You want a ball player, not a nice guy."

"Oh, we're not that kind of team."

"Yeah, that's one of your problems."

"Maybe. But the guys all have fun together. Even when they're fighting."

"And losing."

"True," Roger said, "but we don't break up. Everyone always shows up for a new season. Beneath it all, there's a good spirit on the Miller Laundries."

"Be better if the spirit was worse and the baseball was better."

Roger smiled. "I can see your point. But you're going to California, and you don't care."

"That's right."

"I do. I just hope we're not counting too much on Tony Spain."

"What've you got to lose? Nothing else has worked."

"You're right." He looked at me. We were alongside my house. Every morning including Sunday Roger delivered a newspaper here. From a moving bicycle. Come to think of it, Roger had a better arm for throwing a newspaper than he did for throwing a baseball. He never missed our screen door.

"Bill, you don't think if we get Tony Spain, he's going to mind my being captain and all that?"

So that was it. Truth will out. Roger, our captain, was worried that a really good ball player would nudge him out of his exalted position.

I restrained a desire to laugh. I put on a solemn face. "Heck no, Rog. Willie Soames and Doc Overmeyer don't mind, do they?"

"No. And you don't either. And you're better than they are."

His face brightened. That was all he had been worried about, his status as captain. What a team. What a lack of future this team had.

"You'll be all right, Rog. And don't worry about this Spain. If he acts up, I'll take him down a peg."

Roger laughed. "Now don't do that. He'll be

down a lot of pegs the minute he sees us play. I'll see you tomorrow."

"Right. Take it easy. And don't make too much noise with the newspaper."

Sometimes Roger threw the *Free Press* a little too hard. It hit the screen door, which wasn't always latched right, and whacked it shut with a noise that echoed throughout the house.

"See you, Bill."

"See you, Roger."

I went up our front walk. Through the living room window I could see Mom and Dad reading different parts of the newspaper. Behind them, in the dining room, the table was set for three. They hadn't eaten. They were waiting for me. Usually this meant something was up, something had to be discussed at the dinner table. Maybe we'd be leaving for California before July first. I hoped so. There was nothing like a rainy-day practice with the Miller Laundries to make you want to leave town early.

4

"HOW DID IT GO, BILL?" Dad asked.

"Lousy, as usual."

"They can't always be that bad."

"Come and watch sometime."

Dad smiled. "I'd like to, but things have got very busy for me at the store. Mr. Mahaffey's leaving. . . ."

Mr. Mahaffey was the store manager. I should have been warned, but I wasn't.

"Where's he going?"

I saw Mom flash a look at Dad, who smoothly shifted gears. "You go up and wash, and we'll sit and eat and talk about things," he said.

Now I got the warning.

"What things?"

"Go and wash off first. You're a mess."

"The field was muddy. Mr. Benz thinks you can play baseball in the mud. The ball weighed a ton. I wouldn't be surprised if a lot of guys got sore arms. He's got to be the dumbest coach in America."

"Bill, I don't like to hear you talk like that. Coaching kids is hard work. It takes a lot of time. Mr. Benz is a nice man. And just between you and me, I'd rather you had a coach who is a nice guy than a hard-nosed yokel who knows a lot and would like to be coaching professionally somewhere."

"But who doesn't know that much," Mom put in.

"Right," Dad said.

"You two are a real team."

Mom laughed. "And you're filthy. Get rid of that Michigan mud, will you?"

"OK. At least that's one thing I won't have to do in California."

"What's that?"

"Wash off Michigan mud."

I was testing them without even knowing I was doing it. Warning signals trip all kinds of subconscious reactions.

"Mud's mud wherever you find it. Go up and wash and change your clothes. Now!"

Unlike Mr. Benz, Dad could put something extra into his voice. That extra made you move. I took the steps two at a time, threw my glove and shoes onto the closet floor, got undressed to my underpants, and went into the bathroom. I ran hot water and took a good wash. I really was dirty. I changed the water in the bowl twice, and even then I was scared to use a towel. But I did, and not too much dirt got onto the towel. I threw my baseball undershirt down the laundry chute, changed into a clean T-shirt, put on jeans and socks, and went downstairs.

"Hmmm," Mom said. "A new boy."

"Not quite," Dad said.

"What do you mean?" I protested.

"Look at those elbows."

"Oh, Bill," Mom said, looking at my elbows, "that's disgusting."

I tried to look at my elbows, but it's hard to see the tips of your own elbows, so I went into the living room and over to the mirror above the fireplace and held my elbows up to it. They were still muddy.

"Go wash them," Mom said.

"Aw, I don't eat with my elbows."

"But your mom and I have to look at them while we eat. Wash them downstairs."

"Boy, what a fuss."

I went to the downstairs bathroom and washed my elbows. I was probably the only kid in America who had to wash his elbows before eating. I came back and held them up for inspection.

"Very good," Dad said.

"Best elbows I've seen today," Mom said. "Sit down."

"Well, what's it all about?"

No one answered me. Mom took the lid off the pot of stew and the steam rose. She served Dad first and then me. We were a small family. There were times I wished I had brothers and sisters. No, not sisters. They could be a pain, I heard. But I wished I had an older brother. Back home, lots of the guys on the team were younger brothers, and you knew one of the reasons they were so good was because they had older brothers who'd showed them things. Little things that could become big things in the heat of the moment. How to tuck your leg under you when you slid into second so you could get right up and be ready to run to third in case of an overthrow or a missed ball. Older brothers taught you jump shots in basketball, how to pass and punt in football. You saved a lot of time with an older brother. Well, I didn't have one, and that was that.

"Did you help Mr. Benz pick someone for your team?" Mom asked.

"Yeah."

"Who?"

"A miracle man named Tony Spain."

"Tony Spain," Mom said. "What a marvelous name."

"What's so marvelous about it? And what are we supposed to talk about?"

"I think it's a very romantic name. I've always thought people with country names were lucky."

"Like Max Germany," Dad said.

"Ha," Mom said.

I laughed. "C'mon, c'mon, what's it about?"

"First, I want to hear some more about this Spain boy," Dad said. "Is he supposed to be good?"

I stared at Dad. Why the stalling?

Then I shrugged. I'd have to go along with them for a while. "He's supposed to be really great. He pitches, hits, runs, fields; he steals, coaches, sells tickets, and what else is there?"

"Is he for real?"

"They say he is."

"He sounds like he could make your California team."

"I've got to see it to believe it."

"Suppose he is that good. He could make your team a real winner. Especially if he's a pitcher."

"Dad, first of all, we don't have him yet. Second, he'd have to be able to pitch every game of the season to make us winners. League rules don't let one kid pitch every game. You know that. The guy may be good, but this team will never be a winner, with him or without him. The only winning team I'm going to play on is my team back home."

"Is it that important to play on a winning team?" Mom asked.

I looked at her. "What's going on?" I said.

"Bill," Dad said, and now the stalling was over. I sensed something awful about to happen. Part of me suddenly wished the stalling would go on, so that I wouldn't have to hear the words that came next.

"Bill," Dad repeated, "I've been offered the store manager's job here."

It was out. Bang. Just like that. They could make all the promises they wanted. I could count cracks all winter, and then, all of a sudden, "I've been offered the store manager's job here."

I found myself pretending that what my dad was telling me didn't amount to much.

"Heck," I said, trying to keep casual, "get them to offer you the store manager's job back home."

"They haven't, and they won't. They've offered it to me here, Bill, and if I don't take it, I might as well kiss my future good-bye in this company."

The words pounded down on me as if they were driven by a huge hammer. "Kiss my future good-bye."

"Dad, we've got to go back home. You promised me we'd be going back home."

"I know I did, Bill."

"You have to keep your promise. I hate it here. I don't want to live here. Mom doesn't like it here either. She's always complaining about the cold, aren't you, Mom?"

"I'm not crazy about the winters here, Bill, but this is a great opportunity for your father."

"California's full of great opportunities, Mom. People are always moving to California. In school last week Mrs. Kutcher brought in a map of what states are gaining people and what states are losing people. California's gaining people and Michigan's losing them."

Dad smiled. "You don't like being a nonconformist, huh?"

"Don't make a joke out of it, Dad. You promised."

"I know I did, Bill. If you think even discussing this is easy for me, you're crazy."

"Let's not discuss it, then. Just tell Mr. Mahaffey you're very sorry but you don't want the job and we're going back to California."

Dad sighed. "It's great to be eleven years old, isn't it?"

"No, it's not. It's terrible. You're pulled away from your friends and taken to a cold state, and when spring comes it rains all the time, and you're on a ball club with a bunch of stumblebums. That's what it's like to be eleven years old."

Mom smiled. "He does make it sound awful."

"It is awful. And don't make a joke out of it, either."

"I'm not making a joke out of it, Bill."

"Yes, you are. And Dad is too. You promised me we were going back to California, and now you're backing out on it."

"Bill, be realistic. This opportunity in the company won't come up again for your father. You don't turn down big promotions."

"Then change companies."

"Bill, changing jobs isn't like changing socks. It's a big thing. And your father isn't that young anymore. After a certain age—"

"Hey," Dad said, "I'm not that old, either. I'm not sure I like the way the conversation's going. Let's change it."

"Let's not."

"Easy, Buster."

I hit the brakes. When you get down to the nub of it, there's always the "Easy, Buster," followed by, "You're only a kid, we'll make the decisions here. When you start paying for your room and board . . ." I'd heard that line before. When you start hearing it, the battle is lost, the war is over, and you're on the sidelines, dead.

There was a silence. The stew had not been eaten. I'd lost my appetite. I was angry and hurt. I knew why kids run away from home.

"Look," Dad said, and his voice was easier, "I didn't tell Mr. Mahaffey I'd take it. I just said I was flattered and proud. I knew you'd be upset, Bill. And I knew I'd promised you we'd be going back to California. So nothing's final. He's given me till Monday to come up with an answer. He was a little surprised that I didn't say yes right away. But it's all got to be cleared with the main office. I told him we were a small family and a decision like this on my part cut deeply for the rest of us. He understood. Monday morning I tell him, and Monday he calls the main office with my decision. So, let's eat a little."

"What's going to happen between now and Monday?" I said.

Dad looked at me. "I don't know. Talk, thinking."

"But when it gets right down to it, you say we're staying here, and that's it. Right?"

"Wrong."

Mom was looking at Dad, and I knew this was surprising her. It was surprising me too. It made me fell funny, guilty for all my bad thoughts.

"Fact is, Bill, a promise is a promise. And if it's really a terrible thing for you to stay here . . . well, I might just tell Mr. Mahaffey, 'Thank you for your confidence in me, but I guess my family wants to go back to California.' "

"I might want to stay here, Dave," Mom said.

Dad smiled. "Well, that's to be considered too. It's a big promotion, a big raise in salary, a big step up in my future with the company. But as Bill says, there are other companies and other futures. And I'm not that old, Helen."

Mom laughed. "I didn't say you were."

"You were about to."

"I'm sorry."

"Forgiven and forgotten. Let's have some Grace." Dad put his head down. "We thank thee, O Lord, for this food, and for the good health you have kept us in. And for the happiness that we have, we also give thanks."

I put my head down and started to eat. The phone rang.

"I hate people who call at dinnertime," Mom said.

"Would you get it, Bill?"

"Tell them I'll call back," Mom said. She always assumed phone calls were for her.

I answered the phone.

"Bill?"

"Yeah."

"Roger."

"Yeah."

"We got him."

"Who?"

"Spain. Tony Spain. Mr. Benz just called me. He won the coin flip and got him, and Tony's going to play for us. Mr. Benz called him up. Isn't it great?"

"Yeah."

"What's the matter? You sound awful. Oh, I know. You don't care. You're going to California. Well, anyway, I'm calling everyone, so I called you. Listen, Mr. Benz decided to have a practice tomorrow, and he got a field reserved at Vets' for nine thirty. Diamond One. Tony Spain's going to be there. Can you make it?"

I could. But suddenly I decided I couldn't. "No."

"Why not?"

"'Cause I can't. Look, Roger, I'm eating now."

"My dad can give you a ride there."

"I can't go."

"C'mon, Bill. Even if you're only going to play one game with us, we want to look as good as we can for Tony tomorrow. We could go all the way with him, and every game counts. What do you say?"

"No. I got to hang up."

"Diamond One at nine thirty at Vets' if you change your mind."

"I won't change my mind. And don't bang the paper in the morning, I'm going to sleep late."

I hung up.

"What did Roger want?" Mom asked.

"Mr. Benz won the coin toss and we got the hot-shot Tony Spain."

"That's marvelous. Are you having a practice tomorrow?"

"They are."

"Why not you?"

"I don't feel like it."

Dad looked at me. "That's the first time I ever heard you say you didn't feel like playing baseball."

"With those guys it's not baseball."

"The new boy might make a difference."

"Impossible."

"You never know."

"I know. Anyway, I'm not going. I'll shoot baskets or maybe kick a football around."

Dad and Mom looked grim. I guess they thought I was trying to punish them about the California business. By denying myself baseball. Even lousy baseball. The truth is, of course, even lousy baseball is better than no baseball.

"Let's eat," Dad said, and we started to eat. We ate in silence, which is what we should have done from the beginning.

5

ROGER MARTILLA had his revenge the next morning. The *Free Press* hit our screen door hard and woke me up.

I looked out the window. Roger was gone, and it was a gray overcast day. It wasn't raining yet, but it probably would be soon. Another typical Michigan spring day. You could have it. I lay back in bed and looked up at the ceiling. Should I count cracks again? Was it worth it? I could count fourteen cracks fast, but what difference would it make? I found it hard to believe Dad was being truthful with me when he said he might let me make the decision to go. Fathers don't do things that way. But if he was being honest, if he really meant it, I'd make the decision. We'd be going back to California. One thing I knew: You had to be hard-nosed about life if you were going to succeed at it.

I wanted to be a ball player. The best ball was

being played in California. That's where I wanted to be.

"Bill," Mom said, outside my door. She opened it a crack.

"I'm awake. What time is it?"

"Eight thirty." She was all dressed. "I'm going to run your father over to the store and then I'm going to the Farmers' Market. Do you want to get dressed and come with us?"

"No."

"What are you going to do this morning?"

"Mess around."

"What does that mean?"

"Oh, I'll shoot some baskets in the driveway and maybe go over to the park."

"You're not going to your practice, then."

"Nope."

"You don't want to see what this Tony Spain looks like?"

"I'll see him another time."

"You're not curious now?"

"No. What is this? The third degree?"

"I wonder if you aren't afraid he'll be as good as you."

"Oh, for Pete's sake, Mom!"

"Helen," Dad called up the stairs, "we'd better go."

"All right. I'm coming." She turned back to me. "There's juice and cereal."

"I'm all right. I can take care of myself."

"If you do go out, leave us a note where you've gone."

"OK."

She went out the door. She was sore at me for not going to a baseball practice way on the other side of town when it looked like it might rain any minute. Boy, were women difficult. One thing for sure, it would be a long time before I ever got married. I read once that ball playing and married life don't go together. Well, I had some time before I had to worry about that.

I waited in bed till I heard the car leave the driveway. While I waited I looked for cracks. But I only looked for thirteen. I cheated.

I didn't usually make my own breakfast. I didn't usually make my own anything. And this morning was no different. Mom had left a glass of orange juice already poured and a bowl with a box of cereal next to it. If she hadn't worried about milk spoiling, she probably would have left that out too.

I drank the juice, poured the cereal into the bowl, got out the milk and poured that in, put some sugar on top (Dad always put his sugar on first), got out a fat spoon, and ate it. I was still hungry when I finished, but I didn't feel like making eggs. I'd never made eggs. I'd never cooked anything in the kitchen. Cooking was for girls.

I put the milk away and left the dishes in the sink. I went upstairs to my room. I should have made my bed, but I hate making beds. Making beds is even worse than washing dishes, and I don't wash dishes.

I opened my closet door and looked on the floor. There were my baseball shoes, my old glove, a basketball, and a football. I picked up the basketball and went out onto the driveway to shoot some baskets.

It was a dumb driveway for basketball. For one thing, it had big cracks in it from the winter. I'd be dribbling along and then the ball'd hit a crack and away it would fly. The other thing was that there was a big horse chestnut tree on the left side of the driveway, facing the garage, which prevented any long shots from the left side. It was worse late in summer in full leaf, but it was bad enough now. What it did was keep me from working on a left-handed shot, which I didn't mind all that much being prevented from since I wasn't going to be a basketball player anyway.

Back home in California, we had a neat backboard on a carport with no trees around at all to interfere.

I tried a few jump shots. They fell short. The ball hit a puddle between two cracks and got wet. I dribbled it dry. Puddles always lasted a long time on our driveway because it was graded badly. They lasted a long time in the infield at Sampson Park. I wondered if the ball fields out at Vets' where the guys were practicing were dry by now.

They ought to be starting practice pretty soon now, if they were there. Most of the time the guys got there late, but maybe the prospect of playing with Tony Spain would get them there on time.

I tried a few hook shots, first right-handed and then left-handed. My left-handed hooks brushed the tree, so I stuck to the right side of the driveway.

Once the ball hit the rim and bounced off into the bushes next to the house. They were fancy bushes. Mom got mad when the basketball hit them. I reminded her it was only a rented house, but she said, "The bushes don't know that."

I went back to jump shots, but I didn't have it with the basketball that day. I packed it up and went back inside the house and looked at the kitchen clock. Almost nine thirty. The guys were warming up, throwing balls back and forth, probably looking at Spain sideways to see what he looked like. You can tell a lot about a guy just by the way he plays catch.

I went upstairs and threw the basketball back in the closet. I picked up the football. The football would give me an excuse to go over to Sampson Park and see what was doing.

I went outside again and over to the park with the football. The park was full of baseball players. There were at least four nine- and ten-year-old teams playing there, which didn't leave a guy much room to kick a football. I went out past right field on the smaller diamond and punted a few high ones into the elm trees. I trotted and got my ball and kicked it the other way. I wasn't a very good punter. To tell the truth, I wasn't a very good anything except a baseball player.

Once my ball took a wicked bounce and bounced into the infield of a practice game between two ten-year-old teams. The second baseman called time and punted it back to me, a lot better than I kicked it.

"Hey, kid," an adult shouted from the bench, "don't you know it's baseball season?"

"That right?" I said, and punted my ball the other way.

I punted, chased, punted, chased, until I was sick of it. I lay down way past right field and watched the ten-year-olds play. They were pretty awful. All they had to do to get on was hit it on the ground. Their shortstop was OK; he moved pretty well, but he had a patsy of an arm, looping the ball. Spain was also supposed to play shortstop. Usually pitchers double up as third basemen, but I didn't see why a pitcher couldn't also be a shortstop. I wondered if he was pretty good at other sports, or was he just a baseball player?

I wondered what he looked like. Probably a big guy. Maybe not. Maybe stocky like Doc Overmeyer. Maybe a plug-ugly type, gum-chewer, knuckle-brain, born and die a jock. Maybe not. *Maybe . . . maybe you ought to bike over to Vets' and see for yourself what he looks like. You don't have to play. They don't even have to see you at their practice. Vets' is a big big place. Just park the bike a long way off and scout the world's greatest eleven-year-old baseball player.*

I picked up my football and jogged home. I threw the football in the closet, and then on impulse I picked up my glove and baseball shoes. I guess I picked up the baseball stuff because I would have felt funny riding to a ball park without my stuff.

Then I took off. I made sure the back door was locked, and the front door too.

Baseball shoes looped around my neck, my glove tied to the handlebars, I biked from our house to Vets' Park.

It was a long ride to Vets' because I was going from the southeast part of Arborville, where we lived, to the northwest side. My route took me through the heart of the city. Past the university athletic fields on State Street, past the West Side Dairy on Madison Street where Mr. Benz promised to take us for ice cream cones when we won. (He saved a lot of money last year.) Up Madison past the old camera factory, and then north on Huron. It was uphill on Huron until I got to Vets' Park, and then I was perched on top of a big hill looking down on the baseball and softball diamonds.

It was always fun looking down from that big hill. There were six ball diamonds laid out at Vets'. Three were for softball and three were for baseball. At night during the summer it was a real ball game factory, with the lights shining and the white uniforms of the baseball players clashing with the gaily colored softball uniforms on the smaller softball diamonds. There were more spectators at the softball diamonds than at the hardball games. I never understood that. Softball has to be the most boring game invented, especially when guys are windmill pitching so fast you can't see it, and batters can't get around on the pitch, and the third baseman plays ten feet from home plate in a fixed position, and a guy can stretch a swinging bunt into a double because the bases are so close. It's a silly game played by men with pot bellies who smoke cigars and can't run ninety feet or peg a baseball in from the outfield.

Right now though, on a cloudy, overcast, rain-threatening Saturday morning, there wasn't much choice of games to watch. Only one diamond had people on it, and that was the diamond right below me.

On it the Miller Laundry team was having an intrasquad game. I could hardly believe it. I couldn't remember them ever having an intrasquad game. Usually they couldn't get enough players out in a practice to field one team, much less two. But there they were with every position except right field covered. Willie and Doc were on opposing teams so they had to be captains today.

Willie's team was out in the field and Lew Mira, our lefty, was pitching for them. He was even worse than Allie Benz. It would have been fun to sit up on the hill and watch him get bombed. It was like sitting in the bleachers of a major league stadium. The only thing wrong was that from this distance you couldn't really see how awful the Laundries were.

I looked to see if I could spot Spain. I found him right away, at my position, shortstop. From the back, a tall, lanky kid. He wore a gold softball shirt, baseball pants, gold socks. He was playing without a cap and he had kind of longish hair. I wondered why Mr. Benz hadn't put him on the mound and then reminded myself that Mr. Benz was also looking for a shortstop to replace me. This would be interesting. How good was the fabulous Tony Spain at shortstop?

With Terry Driscoll coming to the plate, I didn't think I'd have to wait too long to find out. Terry was a pull hitter, and Lew Mira threw the kind of pitch easily pulled.

I kept a close eye on Tony Spain. He picked up a pebble and threw it away. A gardening shortstop. I was like that too. Our California coach made all the infielders examine the infield. "A pebble can kill you," he used to say. He was right. If Mr. Benz said something like that, he'd probably mean someone could throw a pebble in your eye.

Tony Spain yelled something at Mira. And so did Pecora. It took me a moment to realize that whole team in the field was yelling. They were talking it up. That was new. I couldn't remember a time when the Miller Laundries talked it up for their pitcher or for anyone else.

Lew Mira threw his Sunday pitch, a slow curve that never broke. Terry waited on it and then stepped into it. He drove a line shot over Mira's head and into center. Whoops! It never got to center. Spain must have been moving on the pitch. He dove for the ball, knocked it down, scrambled after it, and—throwing and falling at the same time—he whipped it over to first and got Terry by a step. It was a fantastic play, a play I couldn't have made in a million years. And the guy wasn't even a shortstop. He was a pitcher.

Everything they'd said, then, was right. Tony Spain, from what I'd just seen, could play anywhere. Here, California, the major leagues. Anywhere!

"Way to go, Tony," Pecora shouted.

"What a play."

"We got ourselves a shortstop."

"So long, Taylor, it's good to see you go."

For a second I thought I'd been spotted, but I hadn't been. They were just praising Spain by knocking me. I should have wheeled my bike home and shot some more baskets in the driveway, but I didn't. I couldn't. Now that I was finally a spectator to this team, I couldn't take my eyes off them.

Art Watkins, a substitute, was up next. He took a couple of bad pitches and then lifted a long routine fly ball to Heymann in center. Harry caught it and threw it back in to Spain who whipped it to Pecora, and around the horn it went, the guys really putting zip into their throws. It was like our infield back in California.

Roger Martilla was up next. He grounded one into the hole between third and short. Tony gloved it easily and whipped it sidearm across the diamond. Roger was out by three steps. Spain was a natural shortstop. They didn't need me one bit. It made leaving easier.

And that was when I should have left my observation point, with that third out. But someone on the field saw me.

"Hey, isn't that Bill Taylor?"

"Where?"

"Up on the hill."

"Hey, Taylor, come on down."

"Come on, Bill. Hit the pedals."

"Let's go, Billy. We need a shortstop too," Doc yelled.

I'd do it for Doc. One ball player helped out another. I pushed off on my bike, coasted down the hill, bumping hard across center field, and picking up steam I missed Driscoll by a few feet, making him dodge. Then I hit the pedals, skirting second base by inches. Everyone was watching me, astonished. I hoped Spain was watching too. I hit the brakes and came to a screeching halt by the bench.

"Hey, check the hot dog."

"Like he's arriving from the bull pen."

"Taylor, you're a hood."

"And a showoff too."

Tony Spain had noticed me, all right, and for the first time I got a good look at him. He was tall, a little taller than me. He had an easy kind of face, grin around the mouth. It was the kind of face I wanted to like me.

"Bill," Mr. Benz said, "if you're going to California, go. But if you're coming to practices, come on time."

I stared at Mr. Benz. Suddenly he was sounding like a coach.

"All right, you know Tony Spain."

"Hi," I said.

Tony Spain smiled. "Hi."

"Bill, you get out and take shortstop for Doc's team. Roger, move to third. Berberian, you play second. Art, get out in left field. OK, who's up?"

"Heymann made the last out," Pecora said. "I'm up."

I ran out to shortstop. Roger had moved to third. A sub named Dick Marshall was playing first. Jack Berberian was on second, and Art Watkins, who

57

usually went to camp a week after the season started, had moved into left field.

"Bill, look alive," Dick Marshall yelled as he rolled a practice ball across the infield to me. I barehanded it and fired it sidearm to first. I looked to see if Spain was watching me. He was. He was swinging a couple of bats, and when our eyes met, he nodded, just a little. He knew; I knew. It was one of those things. We were both ball players. If he wanted shortstop, I'd fight him for it. And vice versa. Of course, I was going away. . . .

"Bring it down, Doc," Mr. Benz called out. "Who's covering second?"

"I am," I said.

"That's good," Jack Berberian said. I took the throw from Doc, and we tossed it around the infield. Roger gave Allie Benz the ball.

"No batter, big Allie. It's only Stan Pecora," Roger called out.

Pecora grinned, waved a choked bat. He took a wide open stance. Doc and I had the same thought. Doc gave it voice: "Watch the bunt, Rog."

Allie was easy to bunt on. The only trouble was, if you squared around too early, the ball took so long getting there that everyone saw what you were up to and came charging in.

Pecora squared around early. Roger charged in. The ball floated up there. At the last second, Pecora drew his bat back and chopped at it, hitting it right by a surprised Roger.

I backed him up and fielded the ball. Pecora made his turn at first and held on.

"One on you, Rog," someone on the bench called out.

Roger blushed. Tony Spain was grinning. He walked over to Lew Mira, who was up next, and whispered something to him. Lew nodded. It usually doesn't help to give Mira batting instructions, since he never does anything with the bat. But Mira was acting like he was a hitter. He rubbed dirt on his hands, adjusted his cap.

I had a hunch.

"Move in, Rog," I said quietly.

"Shut up, Bill," Roger snapped. He was upset. I didn't blame him. He'd probably been introduced to Spain as the team captain. He was scared of Spain. He wanted to look good for Spain. He'd just looked bad.

"Look alive, Stan," someone called out to Pecora on first. Pecora nodded and took a long lead.

Allie Benz should have thrown over, but his pick-off throw was so slow that Pecora would have made it to second easily.

Allie threw home. Pecora took off. Mira squared around to bunt. Roger charged in. Mira pulled his bat back. Same thing Pecora had done, but Mira couldn't do it. He sliced a little pop over Roger's head. Roger turned to go back and fell. I was moving that way, figuring we'd have no play at second anyway. I gloved the pop-up, one hand across my body. Easy out. Stan turned and charged back to first. I lobbed it across the diamond to Dick Marshall, and we had an easy double play.

"Lucky," someone yelled.

"Nice play," Tony Spain called to me.

I blushed . . . with pleasure.

Roger pounded his glove. "Thanks for backing me up, Bill."

"That's OK. Rog, you know how slow Allie's pitches are. Make the batter commit himself."

"Now, don't tell me how to play third just because I thanked you."

I shut up. Roger was sore. It was a bad inning for him.

Tony Spain batted right-handed. He looked relaxed up there, bat back, eye on pitcher.

I looked for some tip-off sign. Roger was deep at third. Tony had seen it. Was his right hand inching up on the bat already?

Roger was thinking the same thing. He glanced at me. I nodded. He moved in a couple of feet. Tony squared around. The pitch was high. He pulled his bat back quickly. Ball one. Roger moved in a few more feet. It was suddenly a duel, not between pitcher and batter, but between batter and third baseman. Between a new sensational ball player and our team captain who was scared about the new guy taking over.

Roger was even with the bag.

Allie threw.

Roger came charging in.

Tony's bat flashed. He pulled a hard line drive past Roger, foul by a few feet. A gasp went up. That would have taken Roger's head off if it had gone straight.

Roger laughed. "I thought you were going to bunt, Spain."

"I was going to," Tony said, stepping out of the box, "but I changed my mind."

He grinned at Roger and then at me and stepped back in. Roger went back to his normal fielding position. Allie pumped, rocked, and fired.

Tony bunted. It was a beautiful bunt, and there wasn't a thing Roger could do but run in, pick it up, and shake his head.

While he shook his head, Tony Spain rounded first and headed for second.

"Roger," I screamed, running to second. "Throw it."

Roger froze and Tony Spain slid into second with a bunt double. He was fast. I'd seen him field, I'd seen him hit, and now I'd seen him run. He was everything they said, and I was mad.

"For Pete's sake, Roger, what're you holding the ball for?"

"Sorry, Bill," Roger said, and he tossed the ball to Allie.

"Time, Ump," Tony Spain said, and wiped off

his pants. He looked up at me. "What are my chances of stealing third on Doc?"

"Poor," I said.

He laughed and stepped off second.

"Time," I called. I had an idea.

6

"NO TIME OUTS," Pecora shouted.

"Stall!" Heymann yelled.

I ignored them and went over to the mound to talk to Allie. Tony Spain went back to second.

"Let's make a play on him, Allie."

"I'll never get him, Bill."

"We might."

"I'll throw it away."

"Quit talking like that. He's going anyway. Let him take his big lead. Look at him, but don't throw to the plate. Fake him back to second. Don't throw it. He'll go back. It's no balk not to throw to second. But I'll go back with him. The pitch after that, do the same thing. Don't throw to the plate, fake him back. I'll only cut partway back with him. He'll think by then you're scared to throw. Then the third time, really throw it. I'll be there and he won't. You got it? Two straight fakes and the third time you throw!"

Allie didn't look convinced. "Bill, my dad'll be

sore at me for delaying the game. Then, if I throw it away . . ."

Lots of coaches' kids are more scared of looking bad than of not doing the right thing.

"Allie, if we pick this guy off your dad'll think you're the best thing in baseball pants. C'mon, we can get him. He thinks he's great. Let's teach him a lesson. Remember now, two straight fakes, and the third time fire it at the bag with all you've got. I'll be there. I swear to you I'll be there."

I left the mound before Allie had a chance to object again. I knew he'd go along with it.

"Hey, are you guys exchanging recipes?" Pecora shouted.

"Wouldn't you like to know?" Roger retorted, and he didn't know either.

"OK. Two outs," Doc shouted. "Forget about the guy on second."

Doc couldn't have uttered better words for my plan. It meant Tony Spain might be tempted to take an even longer lead.

And that is what he did. Tony glanced at Jack Berberian, and when he saw Jack standing there half-asleep between first and second, he took a few more steps toward third. He glanced at me. I winked at him. He grinned back at me. Roger edged nervously toward the bag at third. Allie looked in at Doc. Then he looked back at Tony. I broke for the bag. Allie whirled but didn't throw. Tony slid back in. Fake number one.

"Nice slide," I said to him.

"Thanks. You looked pretty good yourself."

I laughed. He dusted his pants. "I'm going on the next pitch, Bill."

"We'll be looking for you."

"Benz won't throw, Tony," Pecora yelled. "Allie's never picked anyone off in his life."

Tony took an even longer lead. Doc yelled at Allie to forget Spain and work on the batter. Allie looked back at Tony, who grinned at him and gave him a thumbs-up signal. I cut for second. Allie whirled. Tony was quick. He was back, without a slide. I stopped. I didn't go back all the way. And, of course, Allie hadn't thrown. Fake number two. The next would be for real. We had him set up now.

"He's got a great motion," Tony said to me. "When does he throw?"

"The next time," I said. "We're just setting you up."

He laughed. He didn't believe me. He took his long lead, almost a third of the way to third. Allie checked him, looked at Doc. Then back at Tony. I broke for second. Allie started to throw to the bag, but Tony, without hesitating, broke for third. Allie tried to hold up his throw but couldn't. The ball slipped out of his fingers and rolled toward Jack Berberian at second. Tony glanced back, saw what had happened, rounded third, and headed for home.

"Home, Jack," I yelled.

Jack came awake slowly. By the time he picked up the ball, Tony Spain had crossed the plate standing up. He'd bunted for a double and stolen two bases.

I was sore. I swore at Berberian. I swore at Allie. I should have sworn at myself too, but I didn't.

Willie popped the next pitch up to first, and the side was out. I passed Spain going in. He grinned at me.

"You should have thrown on the second pitch," he said.

"Nuts to you," I said.

Mr. Benz decided to see what Spain looked like on the pitcher's mound, so he and Mira exchanged positions. You'd have thought it was a stupid move to put a left-hander at shortstop, but Spain made Mr. Benz look like a managerial genius. He struck out practically everyone the rest of the way.

He was fast and he was smart. He never put the same pitch in the same place twice. He caught corners. When he saw a batter leaning, he threw it inside. He also had a change-up that made hitters look foolish.

Marshall was the first to bat against him. Dick took two called strikes, a ball, and then a called third strike.

"Why didn't you swing?" I asked him.

"Can't hit what I can't see," he said.

"He's not that fast," I said.

66

"You go bat and see for yourself."

"Hey, Mr. Benz, when do I bat?"

"After Allie," Mr. Benz said. "How's he look to you?"

I shrugged. "OK, I guess."

Doc swung the bat with the doughnut. He looked down at me. "He looks pretty quick to me."

"Choke up," I suggested.

"Yeah. Maybe."

Berberian hit a crummy foul ball down the first base line before Spain struck him out. Then Doc went up. Doc was a good fast-ball hitter. He crouched far back in the batter's box, almost out of it.

Spain gave him a fast ball outside. Doc was tempted but held back. Then Spain hit the inside corner with a fast ball for a strike.

"Just meet it, Doc. There's nothing on those pitches."

Tony Spain laughed. He pumped, rocked, gave Doc the big motion, and threw a change-up. It fooled Doc. He was way out in front of it. Spain's fourth pitch to Doc was a curve. Doc pulled out of there, and the umpire thumbed him out.

"Whew," Driscoll said. "Did you see that curve?"

Roger nodded. "He's good. He's really good."

We got off the bench to go out in the field.

"I bet he's as good as your buddies in California, Bill."

"Better," I said.

That surprised Roger. He thought I'd be stubborn about that. But it would have been like not admitting the Empire State is a tall building. The guy was the best kid ball player I'd ever seen. But this was only an intrasquad practice game. I had to remember that.

Spain and I crossed paths again.

"Nice chucking," I said.

"Thanks," he said.

As I threw the warm-up ball to Dick Marshall at first base, I thought that it was nice we wouldn't have to worry about Spain on the base paths this inning. We almost did, though. The guys started hitting Allie all over the place. And Spain was on deck when Mira grounded out, Berberian to first, for the third out.

"Who's up, Mr. Benz?"

"Crawford, Benz, Taylor."

"This is the inning," Roger said.

"The last," Mr. Benz said. He looked at his watch. "I've only got the field till eleven thirty, and there's a team waiting to get on."

There was another eleven-year-old team watching our game from behind the parking lot fence.

"Last licks, guys," I said. "Let's get to this guy."

"What do you think I should do, Bill?" Ken Crawford, a substitute outfielder, asked me. "Bunt?"

"Why not? Let's see how quick he moves. Lay it down the third base line."

"He'll be tough to bunt on, Bill," Roger said. "Those high fast balls are mean."

Ken squared around on the first ball and bunted it down the third base line. Chip Mettler, a sub infielder, came charging in. Spain called him off. He picked up the ball with his bare hand and then fired it hard across to Willie at first. It should have been a close play. Tony had him out by six feet.

"The All-American boy," someone said. "He fields bunts too."

"He's got a weakness somewhere," I said. I threw away one of the two bats I was swinging, took the red doughnut from Allie, and slipped it over the end of my bat.

"What do you think I should do, Bill?" Allie asked.

"Swing away."

"I'm gonna bunt. I'll never hit him." Allie looked around to make sure his dad hadn't heard him, but Mr. Benz wasn't even there. He was down the third base line talking to two adults, fathers, who had just arrived. They were all looking at Spain in his gold jersey and gold socks. A golden boy had come to lead the Laundries out of the wilderness. Well, I had to admit that if anyone could do it, this was the guy. He was as good as his advance notices, if not better.

Allie went up to the plate, already a victim, a picture of nonconfidence. Tony toyed with him, fed him an outside curve, an inside fast ball, a change-up. Then, when Pecora yelled that it might rain and to hurry and strike him out, Tony did just that on two quick fast balls.

Allie came back dragging his bat and shaking his head, like he'd come close and been frustrated. "He's awful good."

And you're awful lousy, I thought.

I made up my mind to swing with a choked bat and look for the curve ball. He'd see my choked bat, assume I was trying to time the fast ball, and try to fool me with curves.

Ordinarily, it's not good to go up to the plate thinking. You don't hit balls by outguessing pitchers. You should be ready for anything and trust your eyes and reflexes. But I guess I was as shook up by Tony Spain's wizardry as any of them. Also, I'd been talking up the superiority of California baseball over Michigan baseball so much that now I had to prove something. I had my little plan.

The funny part was, it worked.

Tony gave me his big motion and fed me the curve. It came right at my left hip. I waited for it. It broke and I stepped into it. I drilled a line drive right at Lew Mira, who was playing shortstop. Mira grabbed it for the third and final out.

Tony Spain was looking at me, surprised.

"OK, boys," Mr. Benz said, trotting back from his conference with the fathers. "Let's gather round. Allie, get the equipment together. Hansford, you help him."

I went back to the bench, threw the bat down, and sat down. Tony Spain came over to me. Willie was with him. Spain looked down at me.

"You were waiting for a curve, weren't you?"

"Yeah."

He looked at me curiously. "How'd you figure that out?"

I told him how. He listened and then he laughed. "I'll remember that one. My brother Arnie used to tip me off on guys choking bats. He didn't tip me enough, that's what."

Everyone laughed with him. You could see they'd want to imitate him in all ways. Tall, relaxed, lots of white teeth when he grinned, he could have been a model for a Little League poster.

"All right, boys, sit down."

We all sat down. Mr. Benz was happy. He beamed at us.

"Today, we looked like baseball players."

"Amen," Heymann said happily.

"Let's hope we continue."

"Long as we got Tony," Driscoll said, "we can't miss."

Spain blushed. "Cut it out," he said.

"Better than Weston Gravel," Pecora said. "Huh, Tony?"

"There were some nice guys on that team," Spain said. I liked him for that. He was loyal.

"I know Webber," Roger said.

"He's OK," Tony said.

Roger beamed too.

"All right," Mr. Benz said. "The big thing is, we have a practice game against Michigan Pharmacy on Monday at Sampson Park, four thirty. Who can't be there?"

No one raised his hand. It was going to be a changed ball club, all right.

"Boy, will those guys be in for a surprise. They finished first in our division last year, Tony."

"But not this year."

"We could go all the way."

"Tony pitching, and Bill . . . Hey, Taylor, why don't you talk your family into staying in Michigan?"

Spain looked surprised. He turned to me. "You leaving?"

"We're going back to California."

"Oh," he said.

I thought he looked disappointed. I was flattered.

"Listen," Mr. Benz said, "don't worry about Bill. We'll miss him a lot, but we're going to be a better club this year. A lot better. Monday, four thirty at Sampson, the big diamond."

72

"Mr. Benz, can we have another practice tomorrow?"

"You could," Mr. Benz said, smiling, pleased, "but I've got to go up north."

"Couldn't you leave the equipment bag with Roger, and we could have our own practice?"

"I don't see why not."

"Let's play over at Sampson. Can you make it, Tony?" Pecora asked.

"What time?"

"Not before one. I go to church," Stan said.

"Let's make it one thirty," Roger said. "I'll bring the equipment over."

"Way to go, Cappy," Driscoll said.

Roger blushed.

Tony Spain looked at him curiously.

"I'm kind of the captain," Roger said, and everyone laughed.

"Item number two, boys. The league fee. I'll need three dollars from each of you by next Friday."

"Three dollars?"

"It was only a buck last year."

"It was two dollars last year, Heymann."

"This is getting as expensive as hockey," Dick Marshall said.

"Rob your sister's piggy bank," someone suggested.

Tony laughed. I guess he wasn't used to a team of comedians.

"Item three. Uniforms. Who hasn't got a new Miller Laundry shirt? We've got new shirts this year. Red ones."

"Tony hasn't got one."

"Bill Taylor either."

"Bill isn't getting one because he'll only be playing one or maybe two games with us. I'll get one for Tony today. Everyone else, I take it, is OK?"

"I'm not," Jack Berberian said. "I need socks. My socks have holes in them."

"All baseball socks do, dummy. They're to put your fat feet through."

"My feet aren't fat, Heymann. They're big, but they're not fat."

"What size do you take, Jack?"

Doc looked disgusted. "C'mon, c'mon, enough gab. I got to get home."

"Jack," said Mr. Benz, "you bring me your old socks and I'll get you new ones. Tony, I'm going to stop by the equipment room over at Jones School this afternoon and get you your new baseball shirt. If you stop by my house later today, I'll give it to you."

"Where do you live, Coach?"

He was a ball player. Everyone else here called Mr. Benz "Mr. Benz."

"Ten nineteen Baldwin. Right across the street from the park."

"Hey, we'll show you where it is, Tony. Why don't you come over after lunch and we can mess around, hit some, and then we'll take you over to Mr. Benz's."

"Would you like to eat over at my house?" Heymann asked.

It was disgusting how they were falling all over themselves to get in good with Spain.

He shook his head. "I got my own food, home."

Everyone laughed. It was a funny thing to say. Tony looked puzzled, but he laughed good-naturedly when he realized they weren't laughing at him.

"Final item," Mr. Benz said. "Who needs a ride home?"

"My dad's here," Heymann said.

"So's mine," Driscoll said. "We can give rides."

"Let's hump it for the cars," Heymann said.

They all took off fast. All except Tony Spain, me, and Allie Benz. Allie Benz didn't take off because he had the heavy equipment bag to carry. That was the other side of the coin of being the coach's kid. You got to pitch when you weren't a pitcher; you also got to carry the equipment bag.

"Where're you going?" Tony Spain asked me.

"Home. I came on my bike."

"I got a bike here too. Where do you live?"

"Where they do. By Sampson Park. Where do you live?"

"A couple of blocks from here."

My bike was lying on the grass. Tony's was chained to a tree. He unlocked it.

"I guess you don't trust anyone," I said.

"Not in this town," he said. We began riding across the field toward the hill I'd sped down a little while ago.

"Back home we never lock up anything."

"Where's that?"

"California."

"I've never been there."

"It's a great place to live."

"So I hear."

We hit the bottom of the hill and started up. He had a ten-speed. I had a three-speed. He was a few feet ahead of me. I'd have had to stand and pump to catch up to him.

"Who're the ball players on the team beside you and Doc and Willie?"

"That's it."

"That's enough," Tony said, almost thinking aloud. He was yards ahead of me but didn't know it. "If we get good pitching, four guys can carry us. Who else pitches?"

He turned to me. I was way behind him. He slowed up. I pedaled up to him.

He smiled. "You ought to get yourself a ten-speed," he said.

"Can't afford it."

He didn't say anything. "Want to come over to my house?"

"And do what?"

"Shoot baskets."

I hesitated. I was puffing hard. I should have been going home. I just realized I hadn't left a note. I had no idea of the time.

"The way I see it," Tony Spain said, "good ball players got to stick together. You only get good when you play against good guys."

Which was why I was going back to California.

"You play basketball in California?"

"The best kind."

He laughed. "You're on." He hit the pedals and left me behind. But he waited for me at the curb.

"You better follow me, Bill," he said. "It gets a little hairy, the way the cars go here. I know the safe route."

I followed him. Suddenly I realized I would have followed Tony Spain anywhere.

7

WE WENT DOWN one strange street after another. I was in a part of Arborville I'd never been in before. The houses were small and not well cared for. Almost every one needed a paint job. The lawns weren't mowed very close, either. And the cars in front of the houses were old and had lots of rust around the bumpers and rocker panels.

We went right and left and then right again, and suddenly Tony turned his bike into the driveway of a house that really stood out on this block. It was small, like the others, but it had green aluminum siding and the grass was cut close; it looked as neat as a pin.

Tony looked at it proudly. "I take care of it," he said.

"It's real nice."

"Except for the crazy backboard. I put that up myself."

The basket on the backboard was a little crooked, but just the idea that he had done it himself was incredible. I couldn't have put up a back-board in a million years.

"You want to shoot some now?"

"Sure."

"Let's put our bikes in the garage."

I followed him into the garage. Tony started to lock his bike. Inside his own garage he was locking his bike.

"Man, you don't trust anyone, do you?"

"Nope," he said, grinning. "If you've got any sense, you'll lock up too. I'm gonna go and get a basketball. I'll be right out."

I did not lock my bike. I leaned it against his and looked around the garage. There were a lot of old Michigan license plates nailed to a wall, a peg-board with gardening tools, some fertilizer bags on wood planks, a sled, a power mower, a regular hand push mower.

Tony came out of his house. He had a basketball in one hand and two candy bars in the other.

"Have one," he said. "It's instant energy."

"Thanks."

We stood there grinning at each other and ate our candy bars. Then Tony took the wrapper from me and threw it with his own into a garbage can in the garage.

"OK. Now let's shoot some." He tossed me the ball. I threw it up with one hand, leaving my feet just a little. My wrists weren't strong enough to really get up in the air with the ball. Tony fed me the

79

ball again. He kept giving it to me to shoot. I made one out of five shots.

"Hey, you shoot some too," I said, and tossed the ball back to him.

"Thanks," he said, as though I'd done him the biggest favor in the world.

He dribbled and then really jumped and arched a high shot, breaking his wrist like a pro player. His shot didn't go in, but I'd seen enough right there. Tony Spain was a born basketball player.

He jump-shot again and this time arced it lower and with backspin. It swished. Then he passed it back to me and cut for the basket. I bounce-passed to him and he hit with a left-handed lay-up.

"I guess this is your sport too."

He shook his head. "I just play at basketball, Bill. It's fun. Something you can do alone. Shoot."

I took my version of a jump shot.

"Shoot from your head," Tony suggested. He put his wrist right in front of his forehead and shot, breaking his wrist sharply.

"I don't have that strong of a wrist."

"Use your elbow more, then. Do you lift weights?"

"No."

"You should. There's wrist exercises you can do with a pole and a weight attached to a rope that will really strengthen you. I'll show you how to do it. Hey, that's better."

I imitated the way he'd done it and missed the

backboard entirely, but I guess my form was better.

"You got the idea; now you got to keep doing it. That'll strengthen your wrist itself. Just doing it. The idea's to get yourself and the ball as high as you can. And a nice soft shot with some backspin that'll keep it around the hoop in case you miss."

He jumped and shot a soft one. It didn't roll around the hoop. It went right through. Tony laughed, almost embarrassed.

We shot and dribbled for a long time. He showed me a lot of things. How to roll left and right, how to head fake and go. He showed me how to rock back and forth on my pivot foot and then drive. He was fast and he could leap too. I'd never seen anyone as good as he was with a basketball—anyone my age, anyway. But then I'd never seen anyone my age as good as he was with a baseball. And he was tireless. He could have run and twisted and jumped and shot all day. I ran out of gas and admitted it.

"Tony, I've had it."

"Me too," he said, which obviously wasn't true at all. He stopped playing and stood there and spun the basketball on his index finger. I stared at it. It was a real trick.

"Would you show me how to do that?"

"Sure. It's easy. Watch this."

He spun the ball from his right index finger onto his left index finger, and the ball kept spinning.

"Who taught you that?"

He laughed and caught the ball. "This, no one. I taught myself."

"And those basketball moves too? The rolls?"

"My brother Arnie showed me them. He used to play for the University of Detroit. He lives in Kentucky now. My brother Jack was the baseball player. He taught me a lot about pitching."

"I wish I had an older brother."

"They can get down on you, you know."

"It'd be worth it."

"Are you the oldest?"

"I'm the only."

"Oh." He smiled. "Well, don't feel too bad, Bill, I'm the only now too, 'cause Jack lives in Indiana and Arnie lives in Kentucky. So you and I are in the same boat."

"Would you show me how you throw your curve?"

"Sure. You got a good ball?"

"No."

"I've got a couple of old ones. They've been wet. It's hard to make them move. Tell you what, on our way to the park we'll stop over at Klein and French's and get us a ball. You hungry yet?"

"You bet."

"Me too. Come on in now. I'll cook us up something."

"Won't your folks mind?"

"There's just my dad, and he's not home. He

doesn't mind at all. I do most of the cooking for us."

"You're kidding."

"Why would I kid about that?" We were inside the back door. There were a couple of steps up into the kitchen.

"No reason, except I never heard of an eleven-year-old kid cooking."

Tony laughed. "Heck, I been cooking since I was nine. 'Course, I don't cook fancy. Just hot dogs and hamburgs. But they taste good. How'd you like a couple of dogs?"

"Sure."

"I'll fry us up some."

He put a frying pan on a burner, turned on the stove. Then he put a piece of butter in the pan. I looked around the kitchen. It was as neat as a pin. I wondered what had happened to his mother, but I didn't ask.

"Hey, look at this," Tony said, his head in the re-frigerator. "We got some cold Cokes for a change. Wanna see something?"

I peered in beside him. "Wow," I said. The whole bottom shelf was stacked with cans of beer. There must have been twenty of them at least.

"That's my old man for you," Tony said proudly. "He can put away six cans of beer a night and never feel a thing. He drinks three cans coming home from work. That's how I know he's home. When that third empty hits the driveway." He laughed. "That was just about my first job around the house."

"What's that?"

He put the hot dogs in the frying pan.

"Picking up that third can. You like pickles?"

"Sure."

"And potato chips?"

"You bet."

"Me too. You like your dogs well done?"

"Sure."

"That's the best. Steak's good rare. But hot dogs and pork you ought to cook long."

The good smell of hot dogs cooking began to fill the kitchen. Tony grinned at me. "Like to see my room while we're waiting?"

"Sure."

I realized all I was saying were things like "Sure" and "You bet," but that was how I felt. Everything was new and different and wonderful.

I followed Tony into a living room that was also small and neat. There were clear plastic covers on a couch and two easy chairs. It didn't look like anyone ever sat on them. There was a small table with a two-framed picture: one side was a guy in a sailor's uniform and the other a guy in a football uniform.

Tony saw me looking. He held up the picture. "This guy's my brother Arnie. He was in subs for two years before he went to college. I may go into subs some day. That's Jack. He played for Notre Dame."

"He must have been good."

"At baseball. He got a free ride there for baseball, but the baseball coach had to let him play football too. You don't get many free rides to college for baseball. There's no money in college baseball. That's why I'll probably turn pro after high school."

I stared. I'd never heard a kid my age talk like that, but then he seemed older than me.

"What's your brother Jack do now?"

"He's got a big business in South Bend. He married a rich girl. I may do that too. Jack always said it was just as easy to fall in love with a rich girl as a poor one. That's my mom."

Tony pointed to a picture of a dark-haired woman in a gold frame. It was on the TV set.

"She died when I was five. C'mon upstairs to my room. My old man and I don't do anything in this room except watch TV."

"It sure is clean."

"Thanks. That's my job. I clean the house three times a week. I don't get it dirty in between, either. This way."

I followed him up the stairs and into his room. Tony's room was different from any other room in the house. It was not neat; it was not clean. It was jumping, crawling with things. There were baseball trophies, a bowling trophy, a football, a transistor radio, a fishing rod, a leather basketball (the basketball we'd been playing with outside was a rubber one); there was a portable record player, and tacked on the walls were pictures of different Detroit Tiger and Detroit Lion players. There were hockey pucks, track shoes, a professional slingshot, a BB gun, a couple of yo-yos, a dart game, and a big Frisbee. There were ribbons for winning track events pinned to a cork bulletin board. I'd never seen so much stuff in a little room. It overflowed the walls and the shelves, and there was stuff on his bed—a badminton racket, a kicking tee, a sweatshirt that said: STOLEN FROM THE HARVARD JAIL.

"Too much," I said.

"Great, isn't it?" Tony's eyes were shining. "My old man says he doesn't care what my room looks like as long as I keep my door shut."

"Did you win all those trophies?"

"Some."

"What about the hockey trophies? You play hockey too?"

"No. That's too expensive. Do you know what it costs to play hockey in this town?"

"No."

"A hundred bucks. It costs twenty-five bucks just to join the league. Then there's skates, pads, sticks, and then they hit you for more dough for ice time."

"How'd you get the trophies, then?"

"When no one was looking."

I laughed. I thought he was kidding.

"What about the baseball trophies?"

"Oh, I earned them. And the track ribbons. You run track, Bill?"

"No."

"I'm a sprinter. I don't know what I'll do for a spring sport in high school. I guess double up, if they let me. My brother Arnie says that Elroy Hirsch won a Big Ten long jump and then changed into a baseball uniform under the stands, crossed the track, and beat Notre Dame with a one-hitter— and he hit a triple too."

"Who's Elroy Hirsch?"

"Crazy Legs Hirsch."

"Oh, him. He played a long time ago."

"Yeah, but when you got older brothers, you always hear about the guys who played long ago. Hey, do you want anything?"

"What?"

"Do you want anything? A puck, a trophy . . . anything?"

I couldn't believe what he was saying.

"You mean to keep?"

"Sure. We're friends. Anything I've got is yours. Here, have a puck."

"No, thanks. I don't play hockey."

"You want this basketball?"

I laughed. "Wow. Thanks, but I got one."

"Football?"

"Hey, I'm hungry. Let's go eat."

"Hey, the hot dogs!" He exploded off the bed and was out the door and down the stairs in three strides. Boy, could he move!

I followed him down. There was smoke in the kitchen. Tony was laughing. He had the frying pan in his hand.

"I'm some cook. How do you like burned hot dogs?"

"They're fine."

"I like them that way too. Open that window, will you, Bill? My old man'll wonder what I was doing. There, that's better. The smoke'll clear out in no time. You like mustard and catsup, don't you?"

"Sure."

"They're on the second shelf of the refrigerator. You get them and I'll put the hot dogs out. We don't have rolls."

"Bread's fine."

"I got to buy some rolls. Boy, am I falling apart as a cook."

Tony set out two plates, put two pieces of bread on each plate and then a hot dog apiece. He forked out pickle chips and dumped potato chips on the plates. I put the mustard and the catsup on the table.

"I'll get us some ice for our Cokes. They're cold, but ice makes them last longer."

He got glasses out, filled them with ice, and

poured the Cokes. Then he sat down and we started to eat.

"Good, huh?"

"Very."

"You sure you don't mind it burnt like that? I could fry you up another."

"No, that's fine."

"You want a napkin?"

"Never use them."

"Me neither."

I drank the Coke and ate the hot dog and the potato chips and the pickle chips. It was the best-tasting food I'd ever had in my life.

"You want another Coke?"

"I better not."

"Why not? They're small."

"Food costs money, Tony. Won't your dad be sore?"

"Naw. He doesn't care so long as I don't bug him. He gives me lots of money for food. That's the only thing I get money for. Everything else I got to get myself."

"Is he working today?"

"Yeah. He works six days a week. He's a foreman in the welding section at the Rouge. He welds lots of stuff there that he takes out under his shirt. Stuff to make lamps and things. You ever been to any of the car factories?"

"No."

"That's one nice thing about living in Michigan. You get to go on those factory trips in school. The Rouge is big and noisy. I wouldn't work there if you paid me a million dollars. But my old man likes it."

"What are you gonna do?"

He looked surprised at the question, as though he'd already answered it.

"Play ball. You?"

"Me too."

"You gonna go to college?"

"I don't know. You?"

"Like I told you, if I get a free ride. Arnie and Jack say I will, but if a major league scout offers me a big bonus when I'm in high school, I'm gonna take it. Take it and see the country. I've never been anywhere. Once to Kentucky to visit with Arnie and his wife. You've been around, haven't you?"

"Just California to here."

"That's a lot of ground right there. And you're going back, aren't you?"

I nodded.

"How come?"

I hesitated. "My dad . . . got a temporary job here. He's the assistant manager of Crawford's, out in the shopping center."

"You want to go back?"

Up till now, I thought. I nodded.

"It must be nice there."

"We play ball all year round."

"Organized ball?"

"No, that's just in baseball season."

"Are you on a good team out there?"

"We won the city championship two years in a row."

"They must be good." He hesitated. "You think I could make your California team?"

"You'd be the best ball player on it," I said firmly.

He blushed with pleasure. "Hey, you want another hot dog?"

"No, I'm fine."

"Me too. You want to throw a football around?"

"Sure. But we told the guys we'd meet them over at Sampson and hit some balls."

"That's right, I forgot. And we were going to get us a new baseball so I could teach you to throw a curve. Gimme your dish and glass."

"I'll help."

"It only takes a second. I kind of like doing dishes. I hate making beds, but I don't mind dishes. If you want to dry, there's a towel under the sink."

"Where'll I put the dishes?"

"Back on the table. I'll put them away later."

"This is fun."

Tony laughed. "I'll show you how to cook too, Bill. And shoot baskets."

"That sounds like a pretty good combination."

"Can't be beat," Tony said, and we both laughed.

He washed and I dried, and I couldn't help thinking how pleased my folks would be if they could see me now. Tony was a good influence.

8

AS I LEFT Tony's house, I began a kind of day-dream inside my head. I don't know if other kids can do this, and maybe it's because I don't have any brothers or sisters, but ever since I was little I could sort of make up things inside my head, like real life.

As I rode my bike behind Tony, what I made up was this: I had a friend named Tony Spain. He was a great athlete; he wasn't afraid of anyone or anything. And he liked me. He wanted me to be a friend of his. So we became good friends. I hung out at his house, and he showed me how to throw a curve and how to spin a basketball. In the fall we played football and in winter we went sledding, and he always took off down the hill first, checking it out. In the spring we went fishing, and he showed me how to cast and where the big fish hung out in the Huron River. And in spring we played baseball too. I hit third and he hit fourth, and we made a championship team out of the dumb Miller Laundries. Tony carried us in all the clutch situations.

In this daydream, my folks were suspicious about Tony at first because I was spending so much time with him, but in the end they came to really like him a lot.

Dad said: "He's a great athlete, you can learn a lot from him in every sport."

And Mom said: "I'm delighted you've made such a real friend in Michigan."

And I knew that was part of why they liked him so much, because I was willing to stay in Michigan because of Tony. I was willing to do anything because of Tony.

Oh, it was a lovely dream. And it went on and on as I followed Tony downtown.

"Where're we going?" I called out.

"Klein and French's," he shouted back over his shoulder. "We got to get us a new ball."

I'd forgotten we needed a baseball. Klein and French's was the big sports store on Main Street. They had everything there: hockey equipment, baseball and football and basketball stuff; tennis, golf, and all kinds of equipment, clothes, games. They had rows and rows of trophies. All the leagues and, I think, the university too, ordered their trophies from Klein and French's.

I wondered if Tony had a charge account there. Probably. He'd have things like that. The way he knew how to do just about everything made him seem years older than me.

We turned right on Main Street. It was crowded with cars.

"Let's go up on the sidewalk," Tony said.

"We can get a ticket for that."

Tony laughed. "They don't arrest kids in this town."

"OK, then."

We rode up on the sidewalk. We went past restaurants, music stores, clothing stores, a greeting card store, and pretty soon we were in front of Klein and French's.

"You wait out here."

"How come?"

"I want you to look after the bikes."

"You've got a lock. So have I."

Tony smiled. "Wait out here, Bill."

"OK, but I don't see why."

"Just do me a favor."

"OK, but . . ."

He leaned his bike against a tree, chained it, and locked it around the tree.

"Now why're you doing that? I'm here."

He laughed. "I always lock my bike. This is the biggest rip-off town in America."

"I've never had anything ripped off."

"Hang on, you will. I'll be right out."

I didn't get it. He asked me to stay out here and

look after his bike and then he locked his bike. Didn't he trust me?

I looked in the front window of Klein and French's, but all I could see was that the big sports store was crowded. I waited about five or six minutes. Time enough for him to buy a baseball. Then I got off my bike, unlocked my chain and locked it around Tony's bike, and went into the store.

The first thing you see in Klein and French's are the trophies, which gleam in the overhead light. There are hockey trophies, bowling trophies, tennis trophies, golf trophies, baseball trophies. To the left of the trophies is the hockey section. Even in summer they sell hockey stuff at Klein and French's. Arborville is a big hockey town. Football and basketball are to the right. Behind the trophies is the baseball section.

I elbowed my way past some kids who were looking at the trophies. There were lots of kids and their parents buying bats and looking over gloves. Tony wasn't there. I went over to the basketball section and the football section, and then I saw him. He was looking at a glass counter near the window. On the counter were little things like yoyos, slingshots, compasses, hunting knives. It was a kind of grab-all novelty section.

There were lots of kids looking there too. I came up to Tony.

"Hey, did you buy the ball yet?"

Tony was startled. "I thought you were outside."

"I got tired of waiting. Did you get it?"

"No. Not yet. I wish you had stayed outside."

"It's boring out there. Do you like this stuff?" I pointed to a slingshot.

Tony looked thoughtful. "It's OK. I got one like this."

"I saw it in your room."

"You can hunt rabbits with it."

"Do you?"

"No, but other guys do. Ever use one?"

"Not like that."

"It's pretty strong stuff. Like a real bow and arrow. Go ahead and try it."

"In here?"

"Why not? There's no ammo in it. Just pull the sling back and hit it against the counter."

"Like this?"

I picked up the sling and pulled it back.

"More," he said.

"It's hard."

"Get tough. Let's see some muscle."

I really strained, pulling on it as hard as I could.

He grinned. "Now let it go against the counter."

"Should I?" I gasped.

"Sure. Try it."

I let it go. It went off like a shot. A real explosion. The whole store became silent. Everyone was looking at me. Then a man came running toward me.

I looked for Tony. He was suddenly not there.

The man grabbed me, twisting my arm. His fingers dug into my flesh.

"Hey, you're hurting me."

He looked down at me with hard blue eyes. "What do you think you're doing, boy?"

"I . . . hey, let go."

"Don't you know that's a weapon? You could hurt someone."

"It didn't have anything in it, mister. Please let go."

He didn't let go. "You don't point weapons at people, loaded or unloaded. Now, do you want to buy that? If not, get out of this store."

I tried to squirm loose but couldn't. I looked for Tony. He had disappeared completely.

"Do you want to buy it?"

"No."

"What're you doing here anyway?"

"Just looking."

"What's your name, boy?"

"Bill. Bill Taylor."

"Where do you live?"

I gave him my address. His fingers relaxed a little at that. But his grip still hurt.

"All right, Bill, I'll let you go this time. But if I ever catch you again fooling around with things in the store, scaring people, I'll call a cop on you so fast you won't know what hit you. Now you go on home and don't let me see you in here again unless you're buying something."

He propelled me past people who were staring at me and then pushed me out the front door onto the sidewalk. He shut the door behind me. My arm hurt. My eyes felt teary. It was humiliating, and where was Tony? It wasn't my idea to do that. It was his. And then he'd ducked out on me.

I turned to go to my bike. Tony was leaning against the tree watching me.

"There you are!"

He grinned. "Nice guy, isn't he?"

"Where'd you go?"

"The other way from you."

"Thanks. Thanks a lot. You talk me into doing something and then you take off."

"Aw, Bill, I did it for a reason."

"What reason?" *To save your hide,* I thought.

"Unlock your chain and let us out of here, and don't ever lock your bike to mine again."

"What's wrong with that?"

"It means I can't leave when I want to."

"I thought we were together."

"Yeah, I know you thought that, and we could have been if you'd stayed outside like I told you to."

That didn't make any sense to me.

"C'mon, let's get out of here."

"What's your hurry now? We don't have a baseball. I thought you were going to buy one."

Tony grinned. He put his hand into his pocket and pulled out a new white baseball.

I stared at it. And then at him. And then I knew

what had happened, and why I had snapped that sling. He had stolen the ball. As sure as it was daylight in Michigan and I was sitting on my bike and he was sitting on his, Tony Spain had stolen a baseball. In the confusion, while everyone was staring at me, he had gone and ripped off a base- ball. He was a thief. The things in his room. The trophies he hadn't won. He'd stolen them too. He'd even told me that, and I hadn't believed him.

My head was spinning.

Tony looked at me steadily. "You mad at me?"

I shook my head. I wasn't mad. Just confused.

"Here, take it. It's yours."

"I don't want it."

"You want me to take it back inside?"

He really meant that.

"I don't care."

"Aw, Bill," he said, "we got to have a ball to play with. We don't have a decent one and they got hundreds of balls in there. They'll never even miss it. C'mon, let's go play some baseball."

He put the ball in his pocket, got on his bike, and started pedaling down the street.

I just stood there. I was never so confused in my life. Here was a kid who could do it all, any sport. Who took care of his house. Who cooked and cleaned, and who was nice. Really so nice. And then he stole things.

It was the most confusing thing I'd ever run into.

Tony stopped at the corner of Main and Packard. He turned.

"You coming?"

When I didn't answer, he rode his bike over the curb and took off up Packard toward Sampson Park.

I let him disappear in the traffic, and then I started pedaling that way too. I didn't know what else to do. Besides, that was the way home.

9

I CAUGHT UP with Tony at the corner of Packard and Wells. Actually, I didn't catch up with him. He was waiting on the corner. I didn't see him.

"Look, Bill," he said, "if you want me to go back and return this ball, I will."

I pedaled by him. He rode after me and in a few seconds was alongside.

"What are you so mad for? You didn't rip it off. I did."

"Yeah," I said, "but I helped you, didn't I?"

"You didn't know you were, though."

"What difference does that make?"

"A lot. But if it makes you feel any better, I'll go back and return the ball."

"Aw, forget it."

"Are you still mad?"

"What do you care if I'm mad or not?"

"I care 'cause we're friends. I want to show you how to throw that curve. You'll strike them all out in California with that curve."

"I'm not a pitcher."

"It doesn't hurt to know how to pitch, though. Look, I won't do it again. I promise."

Now I was embarrassed. A little while ago I was thinking he was like an older brother to me. Now I was like an older brother to him. It was pretty confusing.

"Tony, why do you do it at all?"

He was silent for a moment. Then he shrugged. "I guess 'cause I want to have nice things. And it's the only way to get them."

"Can't you buy them?"

"With what?"

I didn't know what to say to that.

"Aw, heck," he said, "I'm not going to do it again. I got enough stuff now. You still sore at me?"

"No."

"Good. Hey, there's Sampson Park. I'll show you how to throw that curve now."

"I better go home first. I don't even know what time it is. I was supposed to leave a note telling my folks if I was going somewhere."

"Tell them it was my fault."

He laughed, and I laughed too, and we biked across Sampson Park, past the soccer field where the kids played before school, past the little diamond, then the big diamond, past the basketball courts and the tennis courts and the little hill down which very small kids sledded in winter. Sampson Park was the best thing about Arborville.

Tony liked the park too. "It's the best park in town. Our class came here for our picnic. We played on that diamond in the ten-year-old league."

"Did you ever pitch here?"

"Sure. See that tree over home plate?"

The tree wasn't over the plate. In fact, its trunk was twenty feet behind the backstop. But it was a big old elm and its branches extended over a little bit of the infield toward the pitcher's mound.

"I once caught a pop-up that bounced through every branch on that tree. I followed it down through the leaves and I dove and caught it. You know what the ump said?"

"He said it was out of play."

"That's right. I wish he'd said it before I caught it." Tony hopped off his bike. "C'mon, I'll show you how to hold it for the curve."

The diamond was empty. The Laundry guys were probably still eating lunch. Maybe it wasn't so late after all. I could take a few more minutes. I jumped off my bike.

Tony held the ball out where I could see his fingers on it. "I grab it here against the seams. I get a better grip that way. Thumb about here, and press tight upward. Then it's just a matter of snapping it off. Elbow wide here, and I break my wrist about here and release here. You stay here, I'll show you."

I was on the mound. He ran behind home plate. "Set?"

"Take it easy. I don't have a catcher's mitt."

"I won't throw it too hard, but you got to have some speed on it to make it break."

"Go ahead."

He threw the curve. It was a beauty.

"You try it now."

I did. Holding the ball the way he showed me. Elbow wide, snapping my wrist. It hurt my arm and it didn't break.

"Come down more overhead."

He threw a nice slow curve back to me. Maybe it was a natural thing.

I tried it again, coming down overhead, but it didn't break.

"That was better," Tony said.

"No, it wasn't."

"Sure it was. Just keep working on it."

I threw the curve a third time, and it still didn't seem to break. It also hurt my elbow.

"Can you throw a fork ball?"

"What's that look like?"

He held the ball up in his hands, two fingers spread wide around the ball.

"Like this."

"What's it do?"

"Not an awful lot, when I throw it. But it's a good control pitch."

105

He wound up and threw a nice straight fast ball down low. Not as fast as the fast ball I'd seen him throw this morning, but it was OK.

"Try it," he said.

I gripped the ball with two fingers wide. For some reason the grip made me come down overhead, with a nice easy unpainful motion.

I threw a low strike.

"Way to chuck. Maybe that's your pitch, Bill."

"Maybe. But what good is it?"

"It's a good low pitch. Guys hit it into the ground all the time. Joe Coleman throws a fork ball, and he does OK with it. I'm working on a screw ball now. You break your wrist the other way from the curve."

He demonstrated, then wound up and threw a pitch that broke a little bit the other way.

"Not so hot," he said, "but when it's working it comes right in on the handle of a batter. You try it."

I did. It broke better than my "natural" curve.

"Hey, hey, hey, you got a fork ball and a screw ball."

I laughed. "What else do you throw?"

"Fast ball and my change-up. I've tried a knuckler, but it doesn't work. It doesn't do anything but hang up there."

"I can't do it either."

"I think maybe you got to have strong nails or something. Or maybe you got to be old. You see how old some of those knuckle ball pitchers in the majors are. Some of those guys are over fifty."

"No one's that old in the majors, Tony."

"Well, pretty close. You can last forever with that pitch as long as the wind is blowing. Those guys do pretty good in the spring but they barely hold on in August."

He knew a lot, I thought. He knew so much.

"Try one."

"It won't work."

"Try it anyway. Don't use your knuckles. Just your nails like this."

He demonstrated. I tried it. I threw a pitch he had to jump five feet in the air to catch.

He laughed. "Your knuckler's like mine. One thing I noticed, Bill, when you're pitching you really want to get your hips around. And that left leg, you want to get that out. I mark a spot where I want my foot to come down. Jack's always telling me you really pitch with your legs. You got to build a foundation for a pitch. That's what he says. Try that old curve again."

I tried the curve, this time extending my stride in front of me. It broke. I couldn't believe it. I could have yelled for joy.

"Hey, hey, hey," Tony yelled, "no batter in there, big Bill." He tossed the ball back to me and went down in a catcher's squat. He didn't have a catcher's mitt, just a glove.

"Burn it in, baby."

He wiggled two fingers.

"What's that?"

"That's your two-fingered curve."

I laughed. I threw it again. This time it didn't break, and it was way off target. Tony knocked it down, scooped it up, and fired it back at me. It stung my hand.

"Hey, take it easy."

"Sorry, Billy boy. I got into it too fast. Let's get this guy. He thinks he's a hitter."

He squatted, and hiding his hand between his thighs, he wiggled one finger.

"That's your one-finger fast ball."

I fired my fast ball. Way high.

He jumped up, caught it, and lobbed it back.

"That's OK, big Bill. This guy is now waiting for a walk."

He wiggled four fingers.

"What's that?"

"Fork ball."

I threw the fork ball the way he showed me. For some reason the only way I could throw it was coming down overhead, the way coaches are always telling pitchers to throw. It was an easy, natural motion, and the ball went straight as an arrow and low into Tony's glove.

"Steerike!" Tony called out, and pegged it like a shot back at my head. He didn't even get up to throw the ball back. He threw it from a squat position. Boy, did he have an arm. He didn't even know he was throwing hard.

"Let's see the old fork again, babes."

I wound up and threw it again, and again it went right into his glove. He hadn't even moved the target.

"Steerike two!"

"Hey, Tony, I think he hit that for a home run."

"Not this guy. A double play grounder if anything." He tossed the ball back to me. "You got a real pitch there, Bill. You work on your fast ball, and between that and the fork and a change-up you could pitch in any league."

"I can't throw the way you can."

"You could if you worked at it. And work on your body. Lift weights and things. I'll give you some weights and show you the exercises. Lifting weights makes you strong around the shoulders and upper arms. But heck, man, you're a natural shortstop. You don't have to pitch unless your team needs you, and if that California team is as good as you say, they must have some good pitchers."

"They do."

It occurred to me I'd said "they" and not "we."

"You stick to shortstop, then. Let's get a bat and hit some."

"I've got one home. Come on home with me."

"I'll wait for you here."

"No. Come on. I live right around the corner. I want you to meet my folks."

"I'll stay here, Bill."

"Aw, Tony, come on."

"No, I'll wait here."

"Don't you at least want to see where I live? I saw your house."

"It's not the same."

"Why isn't it?"

" 'Cause that's not your real house, right? You're going back to California."

"Maybe we won't."

It was out of my mouth before I knew it.

He looked at me, puzzled. I was a little confused myself.

"What do you mean?"

"I . . . don't know. Something might come up. My dad may get a chance to stay here."

"You mean it?"

"Yeah."

"Gee, wouldn't that be great? With you, me, Doc, and Willie . . . we could take the Laundry all the way. And in winter you could get on my basketball team. I got to show you how to spin that ball yet, don't I?"

"Yes." I laughed.

"Hey, you like to go fishing, Bill?"

"I've never done much fishing."

"It's fun. Really fun. I know some good places to fish right around here. We could get to them on our bikes. Past Dixboro Dam is one place and out old Whitmore Lake Road is a pond no one knows about except my brother Arnie and me. Arnie showed me how to dry-fly fish for trout. I'll show you."

"Have you done it?"

"Not over water yet. Fly rods really cost. They can run you over two hundred bucks."

"Wow."

"Arnie and Jack are gonna get together and give me one for Christmas. You and I can share it . . . if you stay."

"I think . . . maybe we can stay. Come on home with me, Tony."

"I'll wait for you here."

"But why?"

"Oh . . ." He looked embarrassed. "Your folks'll be there and folks sometimes don't like me."

"Why not?"

He shrugged. "I don't know. Go 'head. You're wasting time. I'll wait for you here."

"OK, but don't leave."

"I won't."

I jumped on my bike and started into the dirt parking lot behind the elm tree behind the backstop. I hadn't gone thirty feet before I realized I had the baseball in my glove.

I wheeled my bike around.

"Hey, you want the ball?" I called.

Tony was lying on his back, legs up, doing an exercise.

"Bring it back with you," he yelled.

I kept wheeling around and pedaled on home.

There was a strange car in the driveway, but I didn't think anything of it till I opened the door and went inside. My father was there, which was strange to start with, since Saturday afternoon is a busy time at the store. My mother was there too, looking unhappy.

Standing in the living room next to the mantelpiece I saw the reason why my Dad was home and my mother was unhappy.

He was a big man with cold blue eyes. He nodded at me as I came in.

"That's him," he said. "And I'll bet you that's the ball in his glove."

"Come in and sit down, Bill," my father said in a grim voice.

I went in and sat down.

10

SOMETIMES YOU SIZE UP a situation so fast you don't even know you've done it. I knew, without thinking, why the man from Klein and French's was there and what he wanted. And it wasn't the ball, either.

I kept my face blank. But my brain was busy ticking off escape routes for Tony and for me.

"Before we get started," my mother said, "I'd like to know where Bill has been."

I avoided looking at the man from Klein and French's. "I went to the baseball practice at Vets'."

"Weren't you supposed to leave us a note?"

"I'm sorry. I forgot."

"How long did that practice last?"

"I should have called. I went to—" I caught myself just in time. "I went home with one of the guys and we shot baskets, and I ate lunch over at his house."

"Do you have any idea of the time, Bill?"

"No."

"It's almost three o'clock. Bill, you're too old for this kind of thing."

"Mom, I won't do it again."

There was a silence. Mom sat looking at me disapprovingly. And yet, I knew, the worst was yet to come.

Dad cleared his throat. Always a bad sign. Whenever he had bad news to bring up, he cleared his throat.

"I guess it's one thing after another for you today, son. This is Mr. French from Klein and French's, the sports store on Main Street."

"Your son and I have met, Mr. Taylor," Mr. French snapped. "And your boy knows my store pretty well, don't you, Bill?"

It was hard to know how to answer that, or even if Mr. French wanted it answered. All I could think was how lucky it was that Tony hadn't come home with me.

"Don't you, Bill?" he repeated.

I didn't say anything. When you're in a jam, or see one coming up, the best policy is always to keep your mouth shut as long as you can.

"Why don't you tell your parents how we met, Bill?"

Which meant he'd already told them and wanted me to confirm it. I could tell that from how worried my father looked.

Here goes nothing, I thought.

"I went into Klein and French's today to buy a baseball. I—"

"*Buy?* That isn't quite the right word, is it, Bill?" Mr. French had a sneer in his voice.

"Go on, Bill," Dad said quietly.

"I went in there to buy a baseball with this friend of mine. I thought he was going to buy one. He went in ahead of me. The reason we didn't go in together was because he asked me to look after our bikes outside. He was so long coming out that I locked my bike to his and went in to find him. I found him over at the counter where they sell slingshots and yo-yos and stuff like that. I don't know really what happened next, but I guess I was looking at the slingshot and he told me to pull it back and snap the sling against the glass counter. I shouldn't have done it, but I did. Then Mr. French came over and told me that if I wasn't going to buy the slingshot I should get out of the store. I got out. That's all that happened."

"Not quite all," Mr. French said. "Aren't you leaving out an important detail?"

"No, sir."

"Aren't you leaving out the reason *why* you snapped that sling? So that the noise would make everyone in the store look at you while your partner, whose name I notice you've carefully avoided mentioning, would duck away and steal a baseball?"

"No, sir. That's not true. That's not why I did it."

"Isn't it? I see you've got a baseball in your glove. By the looks of it from here, I'd say that ball was new a half hour ago. Unless I miss my guess that's an Official League Ball, cork-lined center, and under that is printed the words 'Made in Haiti.' Can I see your ball, Bill?"

There was nothing to do but toss it to him. I would have liked to throw a fast ball at him. He caught my toss with his wrists together, like little kids do. He may have sold sporting goods, but he never used them.

"What did I tell you!" he exclaimed triumphantly. "Official League Ball and made in Haiti. Would you like to take a look at it?" he asked my father.

"No," Dad said, "I'll take your word for it." Dad turned to me. "What about it, Bill? Why did you snap that sling?"

"Because he asked me to. I didn't know why at the time. I figured it out later when he showed me the ball."

"You realized then that he'd stolen it."

I nodded.

"Did you try to get him to return it?"

I hesitated. Had I tried? Tony had offered to return it. I'd told him to forget it. I didn't want to lose Tony. He said it would be the last time.

I shook my head. "No."

"Can I suggest a reason why your son didn't try

to get his pal to return the ball? Because the two of them needed a ball to play with this afternoon. Isn't that true, Bill?"

"Bill," Mom said, upset, "if you needed money for a baseball you had only to ask me."

"Mom, I thought he had money with him. It wasn't my idea to rip off a ball. I didn't even know he'd done it till afterward. I was as upset as you."

"But you recovered enough to play with it," Mr. French said, holding the ball up. It had a grass stain on it.

"Yes," I said angrily. "I recovered, and I've got money to pay you for your lousy baseball."

"I didn't come here for money."

"What did you come here for, then?"

"Take it easy, Bill," Dad said.

"Tell him to take it easy. I didn't take his baseball. I didn't even know it was being taken. I don't care what you think or what he tells you. I didn't know. Sure, maybe I should have made Tony take it back, but—" I stopped myself.

"Tony who?" Mr. French asked.

Mom and Dad were silent. I knew they knew.

"Tony who?" Mr. French repeated.

I just sat there. All the fire went out of me. I was suddenly scared.

"Bill," Mr. French said, and his voice was smooth and full of fake friendliness, "if you protect your friend by not telling us his name, you're guilty of stealing. The same as he is. You're an accessory to a crime. Look, son, your dad is in the same business I'm in. The retail store business. It's what feeds you and clothes you and puts this roof over your head. When a kid like your friend is allowed to steal from one store, he's going to steal from all stores. He's going to end up stealing from you, Bill."

"No, he won't."

"He already has," Dad said quietly.

I looked at him, astonished.

"He's taken your good name, Bill, and your reputation. If Mr. French chooses to file a complaint, you could be in real trouble with the law."

"About a baseball?"

"Yes, about a baseball."

"What your dad says is absolutely right," Mr. French said. "It isn't a ball that brought me here today, Bill. It's more than that. And your father knows that too, or else he wouldn't have left his busy store to come here. Do you know that kids working alone and in groups have been taking stuff out of stores in Arborville for over two years now? And not just baseballs, but would you believe bats, hockey sticks, even trophies? After you left the store, one of my clerks told me the display ball was missing. I put two and two together, looked up Taylor in the phone directory, found a Taylor on the street you told me, took a chance and came out here. Look, Bill, I didn't come with a police officer and a search warrant. You wouldn't have given me your name if you were a thief. You're not. You're a decent youngster from a good family who got mixed up with a bad kid."

"He's not bad."

"He steals, doesn't he?"

"Yes."

"Don't you think stealing is wrong?"

"Yes."

"Then he's doing something bad. And kids who do bad things are bad kids. Right?"

It sounded right, but it wasn't. I looked at my folks for help, but they were silent.

"Bill," Mr. French said, "now's the time to shed your bad company. And you can start by giving me the boy's name. What is it?"

I didn't answer. I couldn't answer.

"Come on now, son. You know the difference between right and wrong. What's his name? Where does he live?"

"What are you going to do to him?"

"Find out what else he's taken. Maybe this is the first time. If that's so, maybe he'll get off. If he's taken other things, I don't know. It will be a police matter. Kids like that have got to be stopped."

"He told me he wasn't going to take any more things."

"They all say that."

"He's different."

"In your eyes, sure."

"No, he really is." I turned to my father. "He's really different."

"Did you believe him when he told you he wasn't going to steal anymore, Bill?" Dad asked.

"Yes."

"Do you think this ball is the first thing he's stolen?"

I shook my head.

"Then maybe that's not the first lie he's told either."

"I'll be willing to bet," Mr. French put in, "that kid has a house full of stolen goodies. Bill, you've done all you could to protect your so-called buddy. Now let's have his name."

I didn't answer.

"Come on, Bill," Mr. French said.

"Go ahead, son," Dad said.

"I can't, Dad. I can't rat on him."

"It's not ratting, son. It's not even a question of righting a wrong. It's a question of preventing future wrongs."

"But I . . . I couldn't live with it, Dad. Today, I was thinking it might be a good thing to stay in Arborville. Not go back to California. But I couldn't live with it here . . ."

It was unfair what I was doing now—putting pressure on my father, who wanted us to stay here. If anyone was going to tell Mr. French Tony's name, let it be him.

But Dad wouldn't go along. "You'll have to live with that anywhere, Bill. The thing to remember is that you're doing the right thing, not the wrong thing."

"But, Dad, he's my friend. My only real friend here."

How could I get my own father to understand what Tony meant to me? He was going to show me jump shots; he'd already worked on my curve and my fork ball. He had cooked for me and fed me and tried to keep me out of the store. He was like a big brother. He'd stolen that ball only so he could teach me how to throw a curve. It was for me he was getting into trouble. Couldn't Dad, of all people, understand that? I'd give Mr. French twenty dollars for his three-dollar ball. I'd give—but all he wanted was his name. And that I couldn't give.

"Tony Spain," I said.

I got up and ran upstairs and threw myself on my bed and buried my face deep in my pillow.

It wasn't deep enough. I could hear them talking downstairs, but not what they were saying. Then the front door opened and closed. A couple of seconds later I heard Mr. French's car start up and back out of our driveway. I don't know how long I lay there, but after a while I heard the front door open again and some more noise downstairs, and then there was a tap at my door.

"Bill," Dad said.

"Go away."

"Bill, I've got to go back to the store. I want to talk to you first."

"I don't want to talk to you."

He opened the door anyway and came in and sat down on the side of my bed.

"Bill, I know how you feel."

"No, you don't."

"I think I do, son. We've all had to do things like this some time or other. It's not easy. But it's what you had to do."

"No, it wasn't. All I did was get him in trouble. A kid who was really nice to me when he didn't have to be."

"Bill, do you call making you an accomplice in a criminal act being nice to you?"

"I told you he didn't want to do that."

"But someplace along the line he changed his mind, didn't he? He saw how it could go with you helping him, didn't he?"

That was true. But it still didn't make Tony bad.

"And when Mr. French collared you in the store, where was your buddy then?"

"I . . ."

"Outside safe and sound. Letting you take the rap for him."

That was true, but where else could he have been?

"Bill, I don't think he's a friend of yours at all. I think he's a kid who plays ball well and uses other kids."

That wasn't so. What about Tony making those hot dogs and offering me anything in his room, and his wanting us to be friends?

I felt like burying my head in the pillow again and banging the bed. It was so complicated. Why couldn't it be simple? Tony was good. Tony did bad things. But Tony was good.

Dad put his hand on my shoulder. "Bill, get up and wash your face. Some of the boys from your team are downstairs. They gave up waiting for you at the park and want to know if you're coming."

I sat up, alarmed.

"Is . . . ?"

"No, he's not there."

"You don't even know what he looks like."

"I know what Doc, Willie, Roger Martilla, and Lew Mira look like."

"He was at the park when I left."

"Maybe he's still there."

We looked at each other, both thinking the same thing. How could I face Tony and not tell him what had happened?

"You don't have to go to the park, Bill. Just go downstairs."

"Dad, don't you think I ought to tell him what happened?"

Dad was silent. He looked at me. "What would you say to him?"

"Just what happened."

"That you gave his name to Mr. French?"

"Yes."

"You don't have to, Bill. You could let things take their course."

"It wouldn't be right, Dad. No matter what he's done, he's still my friend."

Dad nodded. "Go wash your face and find out what your teammates want. Then decide about Tony."

Dad left. I went into the bathroom, washed my face, and went down the stairs. Pecora, Willie, Doc, Mira, and Roger were sitting there. In Roger's hands was a new Miller Laundry baseball shirt.

"Hey, Bill," he said, "what's going on? Mira saw you and Spain playing in the park. By the time we got there you were both gone. Where's Tony?"

I felt a little relieved to know I didn't have to tell Tony to his face.

"I don't know. I left him there."

"I got his shirt."

"I'll give it to him."

"How're you gonna do that?" Pecora asked.

"I know where he lives."

"How come?"

"I went over to his house after practice. We shot baskets."

"Is he good?"

I nodded.

"Hey, new ball?" Doc asked, taking the baseball out of my glove. Mr. French must have put it back there. I wondered if my father had paid him for it.

"Yours, Taylor?"

I nodded.

"When'd you get it?"

"Today."

"I bet it cost a lot," Pecora said.

You'll never know how much, I thought.

"What do I do with Spain's shirt?" Roger said.

"Just leave it here and don't worry about it."

"Let's go hit the new ball around," Doc said.

"What about Spain?"

"I'll give him a call," I said.

"OK. We'll see you over at the park. You don't mind if we take your ball? We don't have any ball."

"Take it. I'll be right over."

They trooped out the front door. I picked up Tony's new shirt. It said MILLER LAUNDRY on the back in white letters. I took the shirt into the kitchen and laid it over the back of a chair. Then I looked up Tony's name in the telephone book. I had to make this call. It would be the hardest thing I'd ever done in my life, but maybe having his shirt to talk about would make it easier.

125

11

THE PHONE RANG TWICE before it was picked up.

"Yeah." It was a man's voice.

"Is this the Spains'?" The voice sounded too old to belong to Tony's father.

"Yeah," the old voice said.

"Is Tony there?"

"Tony . . . no, he's not here. Wait a second. He's coming in now. Hold on."

He put the phone down. "Tony," I heard him say, "c'mere, you got a phone call."

"Who from, Pop?" I heard Tony ask.

"How do I know?"

"Is it a kid, Pop?"

"Yeah. Who else would it be?"

All this I heard, and I realized Tony was being extra careful. What did he know? He picked up the phone.

"Yeah," he said, like his father.

"It's me. Bill. Bill Taylor."

"Oh."

"Why'd you leave the park?"

He paused. "Um . . ." He *was* being careful. Maybe his father was nearby. "Man," he said, "you took a long time getting back. While I was waiting . . ." He hesitated again. "I saw a certain man drive by."

He didn't have to tell me who he saw drive by.

"So I took off. You know what I mean?"

"Mr. French?"

"That's right. Either him or Mr. Klein. Anyway, it's one of the guys that owns the store. I didn't know what he was doing around there, but I thought I'd better get on home. Did you see him too?"

His father must have gone away; he was talking freely now.

"Yes. I saw him in my house."

"You're kidding."

"No."

"What was he doing there?"

"Looking for me and a baseball."

"How did he know where you lived?"

"I'd given him my name and address in the store."

"What did you do that for?"

"He asked me."

"That's crazy."

"I know."

"Well, what happened?"

"He saw the baseball. He said it was stolen from

the store. He told my folks it was taken while I was fooling with the slingshot. He wanted to know who I'd gone into the store with."

Tony was silent. You could hear the silence between us, like water lapping up on a beach. It came in waves.

"What'd you tell him, Bill?"

"I tried not to. He and my folks went at me . . ."

"You gave him my name?"

"Yes."

"Aw, Bill."

"Tony, I had to. My folks had it figured out. I had to tell him."

"I thought we were friends, Bill."

"We are, Tony. You're my best friend. I didn't want to, but I had to. I didn't have any choice, Tony. I—"

I stopped myself. I was running off at the mouth. It wasn't doing either of us any good.

The silence was there again. At least he hadn't hung up on me. He wasn't mad at me.

"What do you think he's gonna do now, Bill?" Tony asked.

"He said he was going to talk to you."

"Now?"

"I don't know."

"If he was coming straight here now he would have been here already." Tony lowered his voice. "I bet he comes with a cop."

I winced.

"Hey, Bill," he said, and his voice sounded more cheerful, or like he was trying to be more cheerful. "Thanks for warning me. You didn't have to do that."

"Tony, I'm really sorry. I—"

"Heck, man, don't worry about it. I'll make out OK. I'll see you later."

He hung up. I hadn't even got around to telling him about his baseball shirt.

Mom came into the kitchen and I knew she'd been listening from the living room. Listening to my end, trying to guess what he was saying.

"Did you talk to him?" she asked, pretending she knew nothing.

"Yes."

"Then you've done everything you can."

"I sure did. I surely did."

"Bill, I want you to go over to the park and play ball with your friends."

"Mom, I want to take this shirt to him."

"Your friends are waiting for you at the park."

Was she trying to keep me and Tony away from each other?

She read my mind. "Bill, you can take that shirt over to him later. When Dad gets back with the car, he or I will drive you over."

"I don't need a ride. I can get there on my bike."

"I'd rather one of us drove you. Dad will be

home with the car in a little while. Meantime, rather than sitting around the house feeling awful, why don't you go play some ball?"

"But I do feel awful. It's my fault he's in trouble."

"Is it? Did you tell him to steal a baseball? Give me that shirt, I'll hang it up."

She took the shirt from me. There was no dealing with her when she got like this. She just didn't understand that the only reason Tony ripped off that ball was so he could teach me how to throw a curve. He did it for me. It never would have happened if I hadn't asked him to teach me things.

But there was no point discussing Tony with Mom. She wouldn't understand.

I left the house and went back to the park. It was threatening rain again. No one but Miller Laundries would be out playing ball.

There they were. The same bunch that had just left my house: Doc, Willie, Pecora, Mira, and Roger were out there on the big diamond. No one else had joined them. Well, that was understandable. They'd just had a practice this morning. And another practice was scheduled for tomorrow, to be run by Tony, not Mr. Benz. And a practice game was scheduled for Monday. Back in California everyone would take it in stride, but for these guys it was too much baseball. In California, there was no such thing as too much baseball.

Doc was hitting balls around the infield. Roger

was at third; Mira was playing my position. Pecora was at second, and Willie was at first.

Pecora spotted me first. "Hey, Bill, did you get hold of Tony?"

I nodded.

"What happened to him?"

"He had to go home."

"How come?"

"He had something to do."

That was as good an answer as any.

"Is he coming back?"

"I don't know."

"What about tomorrow?" Roger asked. "Can he make the practice tomorrow?"

"I don't know."

They looked at me peculiarly, as though they guessed I was keeping something back from them. It's funny how kids you don't know well, know you.

"That's a lot of 'I don't know's," Roger said.

"What Taylor means is that he doesn't care," Pecora said. "He's going back to California, and that's all that matters to him. Right, Bill?"

"Right," I said.

"You see," Pecora said.

"Ah, shut up, Stan," Doc said. He turned to me. "Wanna get out at short?"

I shook my head. For the first time in my life I was standing on a diamond and not wanting to play ball.

"Forget him, Doc."

"C'mon, Bill," Doc said.

"I don't feel good."

"Take aspirin, man," Willie said. "And some vitamins too."

"Forget Taylor and hit it, Doc," Pecora shouted.

Doc looked at me. "This is your ball, man. Don't you want to play with it?"

"No. You guys can have it."

"For keeps?" Mira asked.

"Yes."

"Hey, how about that?"

"I told you," Pecora said. "He's going back to California. He doesn't care."

I guess I didn't care. I watched them for a few minutes. The sky started to spit a little. Michigan spring again. I turned around and walked back home. I hoped it rained. I hoped it rained hard. I hoped it rained for forty days and forty nights and washed away the whole state of Michigan with its rotten clay diamonds and its rotten store owners.

Almost in answer to my prayer, the rain came down harder. I didn't walk any faster. It felt good.

At the corner of Granger and Ferdon, a car tooted its horn. I turned. It was Dad coming home. He leaned over and cranked down the window. "Where're you going?"

"Home."

"I'll be right there."

It was only a few yards to our house. He turned

into our driveway. I went up the walk and opened the door and threw my glove onto a chair.

"Is that you, Bill?"

"Yes, Mom."

"You're back fast."

"It's raining."

"Oh, no. Not again."

The door opened and Dad came in.

"Rained out again?" he asked.

"Yep."

"I guess this is a tough state for spring training."

"It sure is."

Mom greeted him. "What brings you back so soon, Dave?"

"Bill's problem," Dad said. "I wasn't getting anything done at work. Mahaffey saw that and told me to take the rest of the afternoon off. I guess Bill's problem has become mine too."

"Nonsense," Mom said. "It's nobody's problem but the Spain boy's."

"I'm not so sure." Dad turned to me. "Did you see Tony?"

"He wasn't at the park. But I called him."

"You did?"

"Yes."

"And?"

"I told him what happened. All of it. I told him I gave his name to Mr. French."

Dad was silent. "That took a lot of guts, Bill. I'm proud of you. What did Tony say?"

I suddenly knew it was all-important to Dad that he know how Tony had reacted.

"Well, he wished I hadn't done it, but he understood I had to. He's not mad at me. We're still friends. He's still going to show me things."

Dad sighed. "That settles it."

"That settles what?" Mom asked.

"I want to meet the Spain boy."

"You?"

"Yes, me."

"Why?"

"For a lot of reasons. One, because he's Bill's friend. Two, because Bill wouldn't admire a boy who was just a bad kid. And how he reacted to what Bill told him shows he's not a bad kid. Third, I want to find out what makes boys like Tony Spain do the things they do, if for no other reason than that some day I'll be a store manager, here or in California."

"Dave, you're talking sheer foolishness. You're not a social worker. You're a businessman. You have no obligation to that boy. If you want to drive Bill over so he can give him his baseball shirt, fine, but come right back. I'd like to keep Bill and that boy as far apart as possible."

"You can't always do things like that."

"We can if we move to California."

"So now you want to go back too."

"If it means keeping Bill away from that Spain boy, yes."

"There's a Spain boy everywhere, Helen. You know that."

"No, there isn't," I said. "There's only one Tony Spain."

Dad smiled. "And it's about time I met him. What do you say, Bill? You want to go over there now?"

"Now?"

"What's wrong with now?"

A lot was wrong with now, I thought, but I didn't have the courage to say what.

Dad read my mind again. "Are you worried about Mr. French being there?"

"A little," I conceded.

"Well, he's either come and gone or he hasn't gone there yet. I tell you what, Bill. If we see his car there, we'll turn around and come right home."

I was still unsure. Something made me hesitate. As a rule, it's no good for parents to get mixed up with your friends.

"What do you say, Bill?"

"Suppose you don't like Tony?"

"All right, suppose I don't."

"Then what?"

"I don't have to like him to try to help him."

"Just how are you going to help him, Dave Taylor?" Mom said.

"I don't know. I'll start by meeting his parents."

"His mother's dead."

"Oh. I didn't know. Well, I'd like to meet his father, then. Perhaps we fathers can get together on things like this."

"Dave, you're a meddlesome fool," Mom said flatly. She was really angry. "Nothing but trouble comes from butting into other people's business." She turned on her heel and left the room.

"But it is our business, Helen," Dad called out. "That boy has become our business."

Mom shut the kitchen door behind her.

Dad sighed. He looked at me. "Do you think it's foolish too, Bill?"

I did, but the way he was looking at me, how much he wanted to help—I loved him for that.

"No," I said. "I'll go with you."

"I thought I was going with you," Dad said with a laugh, "but maybe you've got it right at that. Go get the baseball shirt."

I went and got the baseball shirt and we left.

12

WE WENT the way I'd come back from Tony's house. It may have been the long way, but it was a way I knew. It took us past the park. The rain was coming down hard now, and only Pecora, Willie, and Doc were still there playing.

I turned to Dad. "Did you pay Mr. French for that ball?"

"No. I offered to, but he wouldn't accept payment."

"Why not?"

"I don't know. Perhaps because he felt you hadn't stolen it."

We drove down Wells to Packard and waited there for the light to change.

"Is a store insured for a loss like that?"

"I'm sure it is."

"Then it won't cost him anything."

"Oh, yes, it will. When you have enough things stolen, your insurance premiums go up. And if things continue to get stolen, you can't get insurance after a while. You don't get anything for nothing in this world, Bill."

The light changed. We turned right onto Packard.

"Do you think Mr. French called the police?"

"Probably. I don't think he'd be able to enter the Spain house without a search warrant, and he'd be sure to have a policeman with him."

"What will happen to Tony?"

"I don't know. There may be court action on his complaint. They'll confiscate any stolen items they find. Sometimes an agreement can be worked between the store owner and the family to keep it out of court. I don't know, Bill. Every case gets handled differently."

"He's not really a crook, Dad. He takes things, but he's not a crook."

"Why does he take things, Bill?"

"I don't know. He told me he likes nice things. I guess it's the only way he can get them."

We got stopped at the light at Packard and State. The rain came down harder. We watched college students cross in front of our car.

"Doesn't he have money, Bill?"

"To buy food with. He buys all the food for himself and his Dad."

"All of it?"

"Yes. He does the cooking and the cleaning. Dad, he cooked my lunch. I don't think he's got time to get lawn jobs and stuff like that. I don't want to make excuses for him. Maybe there aren't any. All I know is that he's really nice. He steals and he's nice. I just don't get it."

The light changed. We moved forward.

"He tried to keep me out of that store, Dad. He really did. He told me to stay outside on the sidewalk and watch the bikes. I didn't understand. I got impatient and went in to find him. Then, inside, when he saw how he could rip off the ball with me snapping the slingshot, he just told me to do it. He didn't think about it. It was a reflex on his part. Like jumping a grounder. He didn't plan it that way. It just happened. Dad, he didn't want me to get into trouble. He only wanted the ball so he could teach me how to throw a curve. That's what the whole thing was about. He even wanted me to keep the ball. And as for his leaving me in the store with Mr. French, he couldn't have done anything about it. It would just have made it worse if he was there, because he had the baseball on him."

We turned onto Main Street and drove past Klein and French's. Neither of us looked at it. It didn't make any difference now. It was closed. All the stores were closed. Shopping on Main Street was over for Saturday.

"Dad, how are you going to help him?"

"I'm not sure how, Bill. I thought I might offer him a kind of informal job at the store."

"Dad, that would be terrific."

"Now don't get your hopes up. This will have to go through Mr. Mahaffey, but I think there's a good chance things could work out. Whether that will solve things, I don't know. Bill, if I knew how to prevent teenage shoplifting, or any age shoplifting, I guess I'd not only get a promotion to manager of Crawford's, they might even make me president of the company. Teenage shoplifting alone accounts for losses that run into hundreds of thousands of dollars. And it's not just boys, but girls too. In some places girls are more of a problem than boys. If I knew why kids took things, especially nice kids like you say Tony Spain is, kids who're normal in every other way, good athletes who seem to have everything under control, kids whom other kids like and admire—if I knew why they stole and could help them not steal, I'd be a genius. I'd be set in the company for life."

We got stopped by a light at the corner of Main and Huron.

"We turn left here. Did you talk to Mr. Mahaffey about California?"

"No. He's given me another week to make a decision. The job here is mine unless I tell him we want to go back to California."

The light changed. We made a left turn onto Huron and went west.

"Dad . . ." I took a deep breath. "If Tony can get out of this thing all right, I'd be willing to live in Arborville the rest of my life."

"And if Tony can't get out of it all right?"

"I want to go back to California."

"As simple as that."

"Yes."

"And as dumb too. Tony's as poor a reason to stay in Michigan as playing on a good ball club in California is to go back there."

"What's a good reason?"

Dad glanced at me. "Are you serious?"

"Yes."

"Family reasons are good reasons, Bill. You do what's best for people you're part of and who are part of you. When you love people, they become part of your life and you become part of theirs. And you do things for them even before you do things for yourself. Playing on a winning ball club just isn't as important as this family's well-being, Bill. Ball clubs come and go. So do winning seasons. As a matter of fact, I wouldn't be a bit surprised if your team in California wasn't doing half so well without you."

"I would."

"And who's to say you couldn't make the Miller Laundry team a good one yourself?"

"I couldn't."

"You've never really tried. You were just putting in time on that team, Bill, and you know it. If Tony Spain can make winners out of losers, so can you."

"I couldn't, Dad."

"Why not?"

"I just couldn't. I'm not a leader like he is. Tony's big and tough and fearless. He's a standout, Dad. You'll see for yourself."

"I hope so," Dad said. The rain came down. The windshield wipers went squishy-squish-squish-squish in their regular rhythm.

"There's Fremont," I said. "We turn left there."

We turned. And a block later we turned right and then left again. It was the opposite of the way I'd first come to Tony's house from Vets', because then we were headed east on Huron. But I had no trouble. I knew this town better than I thought I did.

In a little while we were in the neighborhood of small, uncared-for houses. They didn't look as bad in the rain.

"It's in the middle of the block, Dad. It's painted green. It's the only nice-looking house there is. Tony takes care of it. There . . . that one."

There was a pickup truck in the driveway where Tony and I had shot baskets. Dad pulled up in front of the house. I could see lights on inside. The rain came down hard. There was just a small overhang over the front door. We'd get wet on our way to it.

Dad looked at me. "You set?" he asked.

"Yes," I said. I tucked Tony's baseball shirt under my shirt to keep it dry.

13

WE JUMPED out of the car and ran through the rain to the front steps and the small overhang. Dad was puffing as he reached the top step, and he was a lot wetter than I was. He rang the doorbell. I took Tony's shirt out and held it in my hand.

We heard footsteps. Then the inner door opened. There was still a screen door between us and shelter. Standing there was an old man. My first thought was that it was Tony's father. My second thought was: *It has to be his grandfather.* My third thought was: *It's his father.*

Tony's father was old, bald, and husky. He looked like Tony. There was that same brown face. But there was no friendly look in the eyes, no readiness to grin around the mouth. He looked tired and he looked tough. He looked like he could drink three cans of beer driving home from work. He looked the opposite of my dad. How were they ever going to talk to each other? We should never have come.

"Yeah?" Mr. Spain said.

A gust of wind blew some rain over us.

"Mr. Spain, my name is Dave Taylor," Dad said in a cheerful voice. "This is my son, Bill, who's a friend of your son Tony. Bill's got a new team shirt for Tony, and I was wondering if we could come in and talk with you for just a few minutes."

Mr. Spain looked at my dad without any expression at all. He didn't smile. Then he looked at the baseball shirt in my hand.

"Keep it," he grunted. "Tony won't need a baseball shirt. He ain't going to be here no more."

I gasped. "No. . . ."

Mr. Spain looked at me for the first time. "That's right. He's all through with baseball."

"I wonder if we could come in and talk about this a little," Dad said.

"Naw," Mr. Spain said. "There ain't no point in your coming in. It's all over. I'm sending Tony to his brother Arnie in Kentucky to bring up. I can't handle him. He steals things. Today, a man who owns a sports store on Main Street comes over with a cop. They even got a search warrant out on my house. I can't keep them out. What do you think they find?"

I felt sick to my stomach. Dad was silent, watching Mr. Spain. Mr. Spain's eyes were elsewhere, past us, reliving the scene.

"They find my Tony's stolen half the guy's store. Half the goddamn store."

He looked at my father and his face got hard. "That's enough sports for me, mister. And it'll be enough for him too. Sports is what got him into trouble. Sure, we got out of this one without him going to the juvenile home. I made a deal with the guy; I'm going to pay for all the stuff and he won't press charges. But I got to do something else. I got to get Tony in with a family where there's a woman in the house. So that's why he's going to Kentucky, where Arnie and his wife can bring him up right. I couldn't do it. I couldn't do it alone. No mother in the house for him. He did what he wanted. You know something, mister, I gave that kid everything. A color TV, food, pop, and he goes and steals things. And what kinds of things, for Pete's sake?"

He looked at us, waiting for an answer, then laughed bitterly. "You think he steals things he needs? No, he steals hockey pucks. What in hell does he need hockey pucks for? He don't even know how to ice skate. You know what else he steals?"

I didn't dare look at Dad. I stared at Mr. Spain's chest. He wore old-fashioned underwear. Little gray hairs stuck through the holes. The rain blew against our legs. I felt my socks getting wet.

"He steals trophies. Trophies, for God's sake. What in hell does he need trophies for? A bowling trophy. He don't even bowl. I'd buy him a dozen tin trophies if he asked for them."

Mr. Spain sighed. "I done my best by that kid. I took him to church every Sunday. Whatever he wanted, I let him have. But he went and stole. No, he's finished with sports. You take that baseball shirt back with you, son. I'm driving Tony down to Kentucky tonight. I'm sorry you got to stand there in the rain, mister, and listen to this, but that's the way it is. There's been enough people in my house today already."

There was movement behind Mr. Spain. It was Tony. He strained to see who his father was talking to. He was still wearing his baseball stuff. Squeezed in next to his father he looked small and slight.

His eyes lit up when he saw me.

"Hey, Bill," he said.

"Tony," I said, "this is my dad. We came over. I've got your baseball shirt. Your dad said . . ."

"It's OK, Bill." He squirmed around the side of his father so we could see each other. "It's gonna be OK, Bill." He winked at me. He was trying to sound sure, but he sounded scared.

"Hey," his father said, "that's enough. I didn't give you permission to interrupt. These people didn't come here to talk with you. They came to talk with me. You get back inside. I got enough trouble from you already." He shoved Tony backward with a slight sweep of his arm.

"I never got luck from this one, mister. Three boys I got. Two are OK. They both got money. But

146

this one is a troublemaker. I don't blame it all on him. It's not his fault. But if he's gonna go on making trouble, he's gonna make it elsewhere. Arnie and his wife, they got a big house down there, and they can keep an eye on him."

"Bill," Tony said, squeezing around again, "are you going to leave too?"

"No," I heard myself saying, "we're going to stay in Arborville."

"That's great. I'll try and get back as soon as—"

"Hey, shut up," his father growled. "You ain't coming back till you learn not to take things that don't belong to you."

Dad cleared his throat. "That's one of the things I wanted to talk with you about, Mr. Spain." The wind blew more rain onto us. "If we could come inside just for a moment, we might talk about how I could work with Tony. You see, I'm going to be the manager of—"

"Mister, no one's going to work with Tony here. He's leaving. That's part of the deal I made with the law. I'm going to get him out of their hair and mine too, what's left of it. You know what it's costing me to pay for all that stuff he took?"

"I didn't take all that stuff, Pop," Tony said. "Some of it I—"

"Shut up," his father said. "I'm not talking to you. You're not paying the bills. I am. Listen, mister, you take care of your family and I'll take care of mine. It looks like you got a nice kid here. You

147

want to keep him nice, you keep him away from my kid. My kid is nothing but trouble. I did my best. I gave him everything except a mother. That I couldn't give him. Well, he's going where he'll be brought up right."

"Bill, I'll be back. I swear I'll be back. You take charge of those guys and turn them into winners. You can do it. You got that natural fork ball. Throw it—ow!"

The crack of Mr. Spain's big hand was loud and sharp. Tony fell backward into the house.

"Hey," Mr. Spain said, "didn't you hear me tell you to shut up? Now you'll shut up."

There was a silence behind him, all around us. Then I heard Tony crying.

"You can see I got my hands full with him," Mr. Spain said wearily. "You take that shirt and give it to some kid who deserves it."

He shut the door. The rain came down. Inside, I could still hear Tony crying.

I ran into the rain. I ran past our car and up the street. The rain drove into my face, but it didn't drive hard enough.

"Bill," Dad shouted. "Bill," he cried, "wait for me. . . ." But I kept running. I wanted to run into something: a wall, a telephone pole, an old man with big hands. . . .

I ran up one street and down another. I didn't know where I was going because I wasn't going anywhere. I wanted to run as far away as possible.

To California, if I could. Finally, heaving and exhausted, I stood on a corner somewhere, leaning against a telephone pole, and cried.

"Bill," Dad said.

He was in the car. He had followed me.

"Get in, Bill," he said quietly.

I got in the car.

Dad looked straight ahead. "I'm sorry, son," he said. "I'm very sorry."

We drove home through the rain.

14

ALL NIGHT LONG it rained. I lay in bed and listened to the water run in the gutters. I couldn't see the cracks in the ceiling in the dark, but they were there. I could look for them in the morning if I wanted to.

Dad and I hadn't talked at all, coming home.

Mom didn't say anything either when we got home. She made me change my clothes. And then we ate dinner quietly. Afterward, I went up to my room and listened to music on my radio. Downstairs, they were talking.

At one point in the evening Mom came up the stairs and asked me if I wanted to watch TV with them. I said no.

"Are you all right, Bill?"

"Yes."

Mom didn't say any "I told you so"s about the visit. She was sorry too.

It wasn't that I felt awful or miserable. It's just that I kept seeing that terrible scene in the rain.

Tony being hit by his father. Tony, who was so big on the diamond and then suddenly so small next to his father. It wasn't fair for someone as nice as Tony to have a father like that. I couldn't stop thinking about it.

Finally I changed into pajamas. It was too early to go to sleep, but when you slept you didn't have to remember things.

But I couldn't sleep. I kept seeing that scene.

There was a tap on my door.

"You awake, Bill?"

"Yes, Dad."

He came in and sat down on the edge of my bed, just the way he'd done this afternoon after Mr. French had left. That seemed a long time ago. I felt like I'd lived through two world wars today.

"You OK?" he asked.

"I don't know. I keep thinking about it."

"So do I."

I looked at Dad. "Why did he hit him like that?"

"I don't think he knew what else to do. He loves Tony."

"Does he?"

"Yes. As much as I love you. And that's a lot."

I didn't say anything. I tried to see how a father who loved a son could hit him.

"It's hard to figure, Bill. There's good and there's bad. You've got to forgive the bad and remember the good."

Was he talking about Mr. Spain? Or about Tony?

I'd never forgive Mr. Spain. There wasn't anything to forgive with Tony.

"I think Tony will be all right. And so will you," Dad said. "Want the shades pulled?"

"No."

"Good night, then, Bill."

"Dad . . ."

"Yes, Bill."

"Thank you for trying to help."

"I'm sorry I couldn't make it turn out better."

"You tried, that's what counts."

"Thanks, Bill. Good night."

He closed the door. I fell asleep soon after. And I dreamed. Not about Tony or his father, but about my friends in California. And the advertising on the fences in the ball parks. And how cool it was in the dugout during the night games, and that good feeling you got when people in the stands called out your name and clapped their hands rhythmically for you to get a hit. The crisp, clean white uniforms that moved over the bright green diamonds under the lights. It was lovely. It was baseball. It wasn't mucking on hard clay Michigan diamonds in the rain.

When I woke up, the rain was over. What woke me was the sun on my face. There hadn't been any sun for weeks, but now it lay warm and bright on my face.

I opened my eyes. The first thing that met my eyes was the cracks on the ceiling.

One, two, three, four . . .

I heard the squeaking sounds of a bicycle coming along our front walk. Going slowly. It was Sunday. On Sunday, Roger rode his bike slowly because he had a bag full of Sunday papers, each of which weighed three times what the daily paper weighed.

Five, six, seven, eight . . .

Roger didn't throw the Sunday paper. It was too thick to fold for throwing. He had to put his kickstand down and walk the paper to our front door and lay it down there. It took Roger five times longer to deliver the Sunday paper than the daily paper.

I heard him put it against our front door.

Nine, ten, eleven, twelve . . .

Then I heard him walk across our lawn. Not back to his bike, but across our lawn. Mom would be mad at him for that. I heard him walk right under my window.

"Bill," he called up quietly.

I looked for the last crack I ought to tick off. Then I sat up and looked out the window.

"Are you awake?" he asked.

"No, I'm asleep."

Roger laughed. "We got a great day for a practice. Did you give Tony his shirt?"

"No."

"Why not? I thought you were going to give it to him."

"He's not going to be on the team."

"What?"

Roger looked as though someone had slapped him.

"Say that again."

"He's gone to Kentucky."

"Kentucky?"

"Yeah."

"What'd he do that for?"

It was too long a story to tell, and Roger wouldn't have understood it anyway.

"He's going to live with his brother for a while."

"For how long?"

"I don't know."

"Bill, what're we going to do? We won't have any team again."

"Sure we will."

"No, we won't. We don't have a pitcher. It'll be Allie Benz all over again."

"I'm going to pitch. Tony showed me how to throw his curve. He taught me how to throw a fork ball. I've got a natural fork ball. And I'm going to work on my stride. I can pitch some."

"You? You're going back to California in two weeks."

"No. We're going to stay here. And we're going to have a good team, Rog. A winning team."

It was just too much for Roger to take in. Tony leaving and me staying. Tony not going to pitch and me going to pitch.

"Bill, I don't know what's going on."

"You do now. Look, the big thing now is for you to remind the guys about our practice today at the park at one. Have you got a ball?"

"I got the equipment bag from Mr. Benz. We ruined the ball you gave us yesterday."

So that was the end of that, I thought.

"Well, bring the equipment bag along. I'll come over to your house and help you carry it. Listen, one more thing. Everyone ought to wear uniforms for today's practice. For all practices."

"Why?"

"If we look like ball players, we'll play like them. Back in California we wore our uniforms in practice, and it helped."

"OK, if you say so. But I still don't understand about Tony."

"You don't have to understand. Just remind the guys about our practice today, and tell them I said to wear their uniforms."

"What about you? You don't have a Miller Laundry shirt."

"I'm going to wear Tony's. I'll see you later, Rog."

I lay down and looked at the ceiling. But I didn't look for cracks. I was all done looking for cracks. There wasn't a crack there that pointed to California. They were all part of Michigan where we lived, and where we played ball.

Tony was gone now, but someday he'd return,

and when he came back he'd find the Miller Laundries had become a winning team. Not without him, but with him. Because as Dad said, when you love people they become part of you . . . always.

Tony would always be part of me. He'd always be part of our team.

This afternoon, at practice, I'd teach Allie Benz the fork ball that Tony Spain had taught me.

About the Author

Alfred Slote, author of STRANGER ON THE BALL CLUB, JAKE, THE BIGGEST VICTORY, MY FATHER, THE COACH, and HANG TOUGH, PAUL MATHER, lives in Ann Arbor, Michigan, where he and his sons have been involved in Little League baseball for several years. In addition to coaching baseball, Mr. Slote has taught English at Williams College and is an avid squash player as well as a writer for young people. His wife and three children are all sports-minded.